T3-BVM-962

"We can manage on our own."

"Sure." Sean's mouth glided down to the curve of her jaw, found the pulse point just below her ear. "But if there's anything I can do to help…"

It wasn't just the suggestion of sex in his voice that loosened her knees and made her go all soft and liquid inside. It was the under-note of humor, the promise of shared fun. As if, as long as he held her, she could shed the worried caretaker with tired eyes who'd taken control of her mirror and become someone else. Someone a gorgeous man in a sleeveless T-shirt could tease and make love with. Someone warm and urgent and alive she might have been once upon a time.

Someone stupid.

She gulped. "I think you've probably done enough."

"Lady," he answered, "I'm just getting started."

Dear Reader,

As the Intimate Moments quarter of our yearlong 20th anniversary promotion draws to a close, we offer you a month so full of reading excitement, you'll hardly know where to start. How about with *Night Shield,* the newest NIGHT TALES title from *New York Times* bestselling author Nora Roberts? As always, Nora delivers characters you'll never forget and a plot guaranteed to keep you turning the pages. And don't miss our special NIGHT TALES reissue, also available this month wherever you buy books.

What next? How about *Night of No Return,* rising star Eileen Wilks's contribution to our in-line continuity, A YEAR OF LOVING DANGEROUSLY? This emotional and suspenseful tale will have you on the edge of your seat—and longing for the next book in the series. As an additional treat this month, we offer you an in-line continuation of our extremely popular out-of-series continuity, 36 HOURS. Bestselling author Susan Mallery kicks things off with *Cinderella for a Night.* You'll love this book, along with the three Intimate Moments novels—and one stand-alone Christmas anthology—that follow it.

Rounding out the month, we have a new book from Beverly Bird, one of the authors who helped define Intimate Moments in its very first month of publication. She's joined by Mary McBride and Virginia Kantra, each of whom contributes a top-notch novel to the month.

Next month, look for a special two-in-one volume by Maggie Shayne and Marilyn Pappano, called *Who Do You Love?* And in November, watch for the debut of our stunning new cover design.

Leslie J. Wainger
Executive Senior Editor

Please address questions and book requests to:
Silhouette Reader Service
U.S.: 3010 Walden Ave., P.O. Box 1325, Buffalo, NY 14269
Canadian: P.O. Box 609, Fort Erie, Ont. L2A 5X3

THE TEMPTATION OF
SEAN MacNEILL
VIRGINIA KANTRA

Silhouette®
INTIMATE™MOMENTS®
Published by Silhouette Books
America's Publisher of Contemporary Romance

To Jean, for giving Lindsey her name (and some of her
attitude); to Drew and Mark, for teaching me lots about guy
stuff; and to Michael, resident handyman and stand-up guy.

Special thanks to Joan Cunningham, for her patience and expert
legal advice, and to Pam Baustian and Judith Stanton,
for advice on everything else.

 SILHOUETTE BOOKS

ISBN 0-373-27102-6

THE TEMPTATION OF SEAN MacNEILL

Copyright © 2000 by Virginia Kantra Ritchey

Visit Silhouette at www.eHarlequin.com

Printed in U.S.A.

Books by Virginia Kantra

Silhouette Intimate Moments

The Reforming of Matthew Dunn #894
The Passion of Patrick MacNeill #906
The Comeback of Con MacNeill #983
The Temptation of Sean MacNeill #1032

VIRGINIA KANTRA

credits her enthusiasm for strong heroes and courageous heroines to a childhood spent devouring fairy tales. After graduating from Northwestern University with honors in English, she shared her love of books as a children's storyteller. She still visits classrooms on Valentine's Day dressed as the Queen of Hearts.

When her youngest child started school, Virginia fulfilled her dream of writing full-time. Her first book, *The Reforming of Matthew Dunn,* won RWA's Golden Heart Award for Best Romantic Suspense, received the Holt Medallion and was nominated by *Romantic Times Magazine* as Best First Series Romance in 1998. Her second book, *The Passion of Patrick MacNeill,* was a Golden Heart finalist and Maggie Award winner, a *Romantic Times Magazine* Top Pick and a winner of a W.I.S.H. hero award.

Virginia is married to her college sweetheart, a musician disguised as an executive. They live in Raleigh, North Carolina, with three children, two cats, a dog and various blue-tailed lizards that live under the siding of their home. Her favorite thing to make for dinner is reservations.

IT'S OUR 20th ANNIVERSARY!
We'll be celebrating all year,
Continuing with these fabulous titles,
On sale in September 2000.

Intimate Moments

NIGHT TALES **#1027 Night Shield**
Nora Roberts

 #1028 Night of No Return
Eileen Wilks

#1029 Cinderella for a Night
Susan Mallery

#1030 I'll Be Seeing You
Beverly Bird

#1031 Bluer Than Velvet
Mary McBride

#1032 The Temptation of Sean MacNeill
Virginia Kantra

Special Edition

 #1345 The M.D. She *Had* To Marry
Christine Rimmer

#1346 Father Most Wanted
Marie Ferrarella

#1347 Gray Wolf's Woman
Peggy Webb

#1348 For His Little Girl
Lucy Gordon

#1349 A Child on the Way
Janis Reams Hudson

 #1350 At the Heart's Command
Patricia McLinn

Desire

 MAN OF THE MONTH **#1315 Slow Waltz Across Texas**
Peggy Moreland

 body & soul **#1316 Rock Solid**
Jennifer Greene

 #1317 The Next Santini Bride
Maureen Child

#1318 Mail-Order Cinderella
Kathryn Jensen

#1319 Lady with a Past
Ryanne Corey

#1320 Doctor for Keeps
Kristi Gold

Romance

 STORKVILLE, USA **#1468 His Expectant Neighbor**
Susan Meier

 THE CHANDLERS Request... **#1469 Marrying Maddy**
Kasey Michaels

#1470 Daddy in Dress Blues
Cathie Linz

 THE CARRAMER CROWN **#1471 The Princess's Proposal**
Valerie Parv

#1472 A Gleam in His Eye
Terry Essig

#1473 The Librarian's Secret Wish
Carol Grace

Chapter 1

There was a strange man in Rachel's bedroom, in Rachel's bed. A naked man, she guessed, by the hard curve of shoulder that showed in the light from the hall. A strange, naked man.

Her mother must be thrilled.

Rachel wasn't. Not at 2:00 a.m. Not after driving half the night with her two children sleeping in the back seat of a rental truck. Desperation and caffeine were the only things keeping her going. At this moment a naked Brad Pitt couldn't have thrilled her.

Heart sinking, she regarded the long, well-muscled body tenting the flowered sheets. What on earth was she supposed to do now? She couldn't put her kids to bed in that firetrap of a spare bedroom. She couldn't even see the room's twin beds beneath the piled cartons. A hotel room—even if she were willing to drag the children another half hour down the road, which she was not—was beyond her means. And waking her mother... No, she couldn't cope with her mother right now.

Bad enough that the break-in had forced her home. She certainly wasn't explaining it to her mother in the middle of the night, as if she were some teenager caught sneaking in after curfew.

The only solution, the only practical, *adult* solution, was to rouse this naked stranger and oust him from the only available bed. Any minute now an accusing Lindsey and a sleepy-eyed Chris would come stumbling up the stairs, and she needed a place to put them.

She cleared her throat. "Excuse me?"

He didn't stir.

She took a cautious step forward. "Hello?"

The stranger shifted onto his back, revealing a three-quarter profile that could have made Penelope abandon her weaving or Juliet forget poor Romeo. A muscled chest, its nudity emphasized by a perfect pattern of dark hair, stretched above the sheet. A small gold hoop like a pirate's winked from his exposed earlobe.

He was young, she noted. Her stomach sank to join her heart in her neatly tied running shoes. Young, unshaven and outrageously good-looking. Oh, help. What was her mother thinking?

She pressed her lips together, light-headed from hunger and trembling with fatigue. After Carmine Bilotti's threats, she should be able to take one half-naked stranger in stride.

She opened the door wider, hoping the light from the hall might wake him. It sliced through the room and fell across the pillow.

The man in her bed opened his eyes. His dark gaze jolted her heartbeat. And then a slow smile curved his wide mouth and he dropped his head back onto the pillow.

"Sweet Mother in Heaven, please don't let me be dreaming." He raised his hand, stopping Rachel's interruption before she could get it properly started. "Or if this is a dream," he continued, "then don't let me wake up. Amen."

"More like a nightmare," Rachel muttered. Control, she reminded herself. There was no point in antagonizing the man. "Please wake up."

"Okay." He propped himself up on one elbow. Mercifully, the sheet stayed in place. She bit her lip. Just how naked was he?

"What can I do for you, beautiful?" he asked. "And if you need suggestions, let me tell you, I am here to help."

Help. Right. Like she could believe that. But she was encouraged by his cheerful offer, all the same.

"Gee, thanks," she said. "Look, I realize it's the middle of the night and all, but would you mind moving to the couch?"

He rubbed his unshaven chin. "Not to disoblige a lady, but why?"

"Well, because I sort of need the bed."

"I'm *sort of* in need of it myself. I've been working all day."

"I've been driving all night."

"In that case—" he slanted her a smile that promised…oh, wicked things "—you're welcome to join me."

For one crazy moment she was tempted to do exactly that, to slip into the warm nest of sheets and hot forgetfulness of sex. She must be losing her mind. From sleep deprivation or stress or something.

"No. Thank you," she added politely. "The bed is for my children."

His eyebrows lifted. His gaze traveled past her to the hall. "And they are...?"

"Downstairs. In the truck."

That broad palm scrubbed his face again. "And you are...?"

"Rachel Fuller." Clearly the name meant nothing to him. She sighed again. "Myra's daughter."

"Rachel? You're Rachel?" Dropping his hand, he inspected her again, reminding her sharply that she was sweaty and grungy and wrinkled. "I thought you weren't due for a couple of days yet."

She lifted her chin. "I didn't think my mother set a time limit on her invitation."

He grinned. "I thought you'd be older."

She dredged a wry smile from somewhere. "I'm ancient," she told him. It felt true. "And very, very tired. And I have two tired, cranky children. So, if you really wouldn't mind, Mr....?"

"Sean. Sean MacNeill." He curled up effortlessly, bunching the sheet at his waist, and extended his big hand.

Rachel took it, feeling the ridiculousness of the formal gesture in the face of her snarled nerves and his near nudity. His grip was sure and strong, his palm calloused. A scar ran across the knuckle of his thumb. He tugged on their joined hands, bringing her face down to his level.

Rachel blinked as his warm breath skated across her mouth. He smelled like toothpaste, like soap and sleep and man.

"Welcome home, Rachel Fuller."

And then his warm lips brushed her cheek.

She felt the bristle of his beard, the softness of his lips. Despite her surprise, under her indignation, her stomach gave a quick undisciplined thump. Alarmed, she pushed against the smooth curve of his shoulder. He released her instantly.

"Get up," she commanded, panicked by the threat to her control.

"Yes, ma'am. As soon as you turn your back. Unless—" his hand hovered above the sheet at his waist "—you'd like to watch?"

Maybe. Oh, Lord. She really was losing her mind. Turning her back, she said in her most daunting schoolteacher's voice, "I hardly think that's appropriate."

She heard the squeak of the mattress behind her, the rustle of sheets. "Just welcoming you home."

He meant the kiss. "That wasn't just inappropriate. That was uncalled for."

Something—a belt buckle?—clanked as he tugged on his jeans. She listened for the reassuring rasp of his zipper, her face hot in the dark. It was unbearably intimate, listening to this large stranger dress behind her.

"Seemed to fit the circumstances to me," he remarked. "Most times a woman wakes me up in the middle of the night, she expects a hell of a lot more than a kiss."

This time she couldn't summon anything in response to his teasing. Not a smile. Not a word. It was as though the break-in had fractured something inside her, her spirit or her sense of humor, that gave way unexpectedly under pressure. She hugged her elbows tighter.

"Hey." His voice gentled. "It's okay."

It wasn't okay, Rachel thought bleakly. Things hadn't been okay for a very long time. The willpower that had held her together through the long drive, and her stripped and vandalized living room before that, and the truly horrible year before that, stretched thin as thread. At the slightest tug she'd unravel like new knitting. She could feel herself fraying already.

But she appreciated his attempt at comfort.

She turned as he reached for the T-shirt draped over the back of her vanity chair, struggling for the normal social responses that would get her through this. "I'm sorry. I wasn't expecting..."

He tugged the shirt over his head. "I said it's okay. Take the bed. I'll clear the rest of my stuff out in the morning."

"I... Thank you." Now that he was moving and dressed, she felt the familiar prick of guilt. "I'll get you a pillow for the couch."

"I'll do it."

So he knew his way around her mother's closets. The thought twinged like a pulled muscle. Rachel's adolescence had been marked by a procession of "uncles"— some intimate, some not-so-intimate, some nice, some not-so-nice—all recruited to alleviate her mother's terrible loneliness after her father died. Rachel didn't really suspect this latest houseguest of visiting her mother's bed. Surely he was too young? But she didn't appreciate finding him in hers, either.

"Fine," she said, and went downstairs and out of the house.

The sultry August night enveloped her. Cicadas buzzed from overgrown azaleas and pines. A troop of moths wandered drunkenly in and out of the light at the corner of the old frame house, sparking like planes in a dogfight. Her athletic shoes crunched on the graveled drive. Despite the muggy heat, Rachel shivered as she approached the parked truck.

In the front seat Chris was awake and still, his pale eyes gleaming in the shadows. Rachel's insides pinched at the apprehensive look on his face. At eight, he was still so young. Too young to deal with his life being turned topsy-turvy. The events of the past year had turned her "easy" baby, her happy child, into this anxious and uncertain boy. More than anything, Rachel longed to set things right again.

At her tap, he uncurled and scrambled to unlock the passenger door.

"Hi, sweetie. We're here."

He nodded.

On the bench seat behind him, ten-year-old Lindsey sprawled, hair and arms and legs every which way. Her lips parted; her dark lashes fanned her cheeks. Sleeping, she looked so much like the sweet baby she had been that Rachel wanted to crawl in and cradle her.

She put her hand on her shoulder instead, knowing that was the most her daughter tolerated these days. "Lindsey? Honey, we're at Grandma's."

Dark eyes opened. "You woke me up."

"Yes. Come on, honey. Let's get you to bed."

"I'm tired."

"I know."

She soothed and prodded the kids from the truck, making sure Lindsey clutched her pillow and Chris his bear. Briefly, Rachel wished she had her own talisman. But she was the grown-up. She was too old for a "blankie." Grabbing the children's duffel bags instead, she shepherded her family along the short walk, promising water and a bathroom and French toast in the morning.

A shadow loomed across the concrete steps as the stranger appeared in the doorway. Backlit, standing, he looked enormous. Rachel stopped, her heart jolting. Chris pressed into her side.

"Give you a hand?" he rumbled.

Rachel drew a deep breath. They were in tiny Benson,

North Carolina, she reminded herself. Miles away from any threat to her children.

She made herself smile. "No, thank you. We're fine."

Lindsey scowled. "Who's he?"

"This is Mr. MacNeill," Rachel said, urging them up the steps.

He stepped back to let them pass, smiling engagingly down at the children. "Call me Sean."

Her daughter's dark brows came together over her nose. "But who *is* he?"

Rachel wished she knew. She was half afraid to find out. "He, um…"

"I work sometimes for your grandmother," the tall man said. "Can I take that upstairs for you?"

Rachel tightened her grip on the duffel strap. "I can do it."

"You can take mine," Lindsey said.

He lifted an eyebrow, glanced at Rachel. And waited. The yellow lamplight winked on the gold earring, making him look even more like a pirate.

"Well… Thank you," she said, and handed their bags over. "The room at the top of the stairs."

"I remember the way."

Silenced, she followed his broad back and long legs up the narrow staircase.

Lindsey, pushing ahead, stopped in the doorway and regarded their accommodations with scorn. "Where are we supposed to sleep?"

Dismay rose in Rachel. "In the bed," she said with forced cheerfulness.

"I'm not sharing a bed with Chris. He farts."

Her brother poked his head around Rachel. "You kick."

"Baby," Lindsey sneered.

Chris tautened with eight-year-old rage and dignity. Rachel squeezed his shoulder in comfort, in warning. "That's quite enough, Lindsey."

The pirate deposited their bags and then propped himself in the doorway. "So, who *do* you want to bunk with?" he asked Lindsey.

Her startled gaze flew to his face.

Rachel's protective instincts went off like a smoke alarm. "Now wait a minute..."

He shrugged. "I'm just pointing out that everybody's got some bad habit. Like they snore or they drool or they steal the covers. You want to take a chance with your grandmother?"

"No..." Lindsey said uncertainly.

"No," he agreed. "I'm betting you don't want to sleep in the car. Your mom's taking the floor, and I'm not offering. So I guess you're sharing a bed with your brother." Straightening, he gave Rachel a brief smile. "Good night."

"Good night," she echoed.

He sauntered down the stairs, his head nearly brushing the canted ceiling.

Well. Had he deliberately baited her daughter to trick her cooperation? Rachel pursed her mouth, unsure how she felt about Tall, Dark and In-Your-Face interfering with her children.

She glanced down at Chris's white face. Both kids were almost swaying on their feet. It would wait until the morning, she decided. Everything could wait until morning.

She was lying on the floor beside the bed, listening to her sleeping children, before it occurred to her that Sean MacNeill never came back for his pillow.

Tiny blue flowers dotted the wallpaper. Rachel always imagined that their scent perfumed the room, and not the lavender sachet her mother put in all the drawers. She snuggled deeper, wrapped in sleep and a light cotton blanket. The smell of coffee and biscuits rose from the kitchen, and the deep sound of her father's laughter.

Two things shattered her morning dream, more or less at once: she was sleeping on the floor, not in her childhood bed, and that laugh didn't belong to her father. Her father had been dead for twenty years. Tears pricked her eyes.

"Damn," she whispered.

Chris rolled over on the mattress above her. "Mom?"

"It's okay, honey," she soothed him. "Go back to sleep."

Doubled over in the early light, she pulled on her jeans and finger-combed her hair. Tears were of no use at all. What she needed—what Lindsey and Chris needed—was a fresh start. A good breakfast, a secure future, and miles between them and Carmine Bilotti's threats.

Don't think about that. Not now. Not, please God, ever again.

She poked her toes into her running shoes. What to do first? She ought to unpack the truck. Clear out the spare bedroom. Find out exactly what Sean MacNeill was doing in her mother's house and...well, she'd figure it out as she went along.

Not for the first time in the past year, she wished crises came with instruction manuals.

Tugging her belt, she marched down the stairs.

Her mother stood at the kitchen sink in a housedress and slippers, washing out a blue-and-white ceramic bowl. Her graying blond hair was already neatly curled. A soft pink lipstick defined her mouth. Unlike her tall, athletic daughter, Myra Jordan would no more go out in public without makeup than without a bra. Sudden affection for her caught Rachel unprepared, swamping her chest. Maybe the adage was wrong, she thought with a little lift of heart. Maybe you could go home again.

Myra's dark-haired houseguest sprawled at the kitchen table, back to the door, bare feet sticking out under the table. With his gold hoop and morning stubble, he looked dangerous, disreputable, and very, very attractive.

Rachel stopped in the kitchen doorway. Then again, home hadn't been a reliable refuge since her father died.

Sean turned one of her mother's flowered coffee mugs in his big hands. "I don't want to put you out, Mrs. Jordan. I'm due on-site in another hour, anyway."

"Oh, it's no trouble. And those biscuits'll be ready in just a minute."

Rachel took a deep breath. "Good morning, Mama."

"Rachel!" Letting the bowl slide into the soapy water, her mother rushed to envelope her in warm, yielding arms and the scent of lemony detergent.

Just for a moment Rachel closed her eyes, holding on to the illusion of homecoming.

"You didn't wake me when you came in," Myra chided.

Rachel leaned back to inspect her mother's soft, lined face. She looked older, Rachel thought, concerned. What if the children were too much for her? Or what if, despite the payment Rachel mailed yesterday, the Bilottis came after them? She'd never forgive herself if she'd put her own mother at risk. But what choice did she have?

"Yes, well…I didn't want to disturb you."

"You've met Sean?"

Dark eyes, bright with mischief, watched her over the rim of his mug. "I welcomed her home," he said gravely. "Then I cleared out so she could tuck the kids in."

Rachel's whole body warmed at the look in his eyes, as if she'd already been for her morning run. Ducking her head to hide her hot cheeks, she poured herself coffee. "Yes, he did. Thank you. For vacating the room," she added, in case he thought she meant the other. That kiss.

He looked amused. He remembered. "Don't mention it."

"You didn't get a pillow," she said foolishly, and then bit her tongue.

"There are pillows on the couch. I figured you and the kids could use what was in the closet."

"I hope you were comfortable," Myra said. To which one of them, Rachel wasn't sure.

"Very comfortable, Mama. Mr.—Sean gave up his bed for the children." My bed, she thought but did not say. "Of course, now that we're here, I'm hoping I can clean up the spare room for them."

"Oh, yes. Yes, of course. I meant to tidy things up before you came. But you're early, dear."

Rachel took a sip of coffee, swallowing the guilt caused by her mother's faint reproach. She'd never planned on coming home. But then, she'd never planned on the Bilottis, either. If it weren't for the threat to her children... There was no way she could pay what she owed and still afford the mortgage on the house she'd shared with Doug. At this moment she couldn't even scrape together a security deposit for an apartment.

"Sorry, Mama. But now that we're here, I can help. We can shift some of those boxes and things into my room until I can go through them."

"Oh, but..." Myra turned, as she always turned in doubt, to the man in the room. Rachel felt the ground shift beneath her feet.

"Your daughter should have her room, Mrs. Jordan. I told you I'd be just fine in the garage."

"But with all you do…"

"What exactly *do* you do, Sean?" Rachel interrupted. His eyes laughed at her. "Whatever you need."

"Sean's a carpenter," Myra explained eagerly. "He's working on that new development outside Buchanan."

"And what is it that you do *here?*" Rachel persisted.

"I keep a few things here."

"He's renting the garage. He came to replace that trim around the window—where it was all rotten, remember? I told you about it on the phone—and he saw all that unused space and asked if I would consider leasing it. So, of course I said yes."

Sean MacNeill had seen something, all right, Rachel thought worriedly. A vulnerable older woman, unattached, unprotected, only too happy to have a personable man around the place. Of course her mother had said yes.

She fretted her lower lip with her teeth, remembering the "uncles." Chris and Lindsey had just lost their father. They'd been torn from their home and their friends. Rachel knew from painful experience that the last thing her bereaved children needed was a fly-by-night attachment to another man who wouldn't stick around.

The oven timer buzzed. Myra bustled to set honey, butter and biscuits on the table. Sean took three.

Rachel arched her eyebrows. "Bed *and* board?"

He grinned at her. "Your mom's a good cook."

Myra sighed. "It's so nice to have a man with an appetite around."

Rachel's throat tightened. Oh, Mama.

He polished off the biscuits and pushed away from the table. "Thanks for breakfast, Mrs. Jordan. Kids up yet?" he asked Rachel. "I need to get my shoes."

His courtesy disarmed her. "No. I'll get them."

"They're by the closet. Somewhere on the floor over there, anyway."

She found them, finally, kicked under the dresser, Sasquatch-size work boots, soles red with clay. Holding them by their laces, she carried them downstairs.

"Thanks," he said briefly, and bent to do them up. "You want to give me your keys?"

"What for?"

He stood. He was tall. She wasn't used to a man she had to look up to. "I've got to move your truck. You're blocking me in."

"Sorry." She didn't feel sorry. She felt displaced. "I'll move it."

She led the way outside. "How long have you been renting from my mother?" she asked as soon as they were out of earshot of the kitchen.

"Not long," he said easily.

She jingled her keys, hurrying to keep pace with his long stride. "It's going to be awkward, negotiating two cars in the driveway."

"I can live with it."

"And there's the problem of space. Bedrooms..."

"Hey, I'm willing to share."

She dipped her head, letting her hair swing forward to hide her smile. "Very generous of you," she said dryly. "But it may be..." She swallowed. *Go on. Say it.* "Maybe now that we're here, it just won't work out."

He stopped, giving her a long, slow once-over from surprisingly shrewd brown eyes. "Maybe. You might want to take that up with your mom. She doesn't like living alone."

"She won't be alone. She has her grandchildren now. She has me."

"Like I said, you should take that up with her." Plucking the keys from her hand, he opened the rental truck's door. His gentlemanly gesture confused her. Put her at a disadvantage. But short of wrestling for the keys, there was nothing she could do.

He handed them back. "Look, I'm not getting in the middle of some family thing. I've got family enough of my own. As far as I'm concerned, your mom is just a nice lady with an empty garage."

"And a cozy house."

That long-boned, laid-back body tensed. "The garage isn't livable yet. I only agreed to stay in the house because your mother said it made her feel safe. But I'm not dogging for anybody to feed me or mother me or keep track of my comings and goings, and I'm sure not looking for hassles." He took a quick, annoyed breath. "Clear?"

"Yes," said Rachel, a bit breathless herself at his unexpected vehemence. Could she believe him? "Thank you, that's very clear."

"Good." He waited until she climbed up into the cab and then closed the driver's side door. "You two talk it over. I'm taking delivery on a new table saw, and I'd kind of like to know where to put it." His wicked grin glimmered. "Don't go jumping in with suggestions, now, beautiful."

Her laugh sputtered, surprising them both. His smile broadened. Softened. Got personal.

"That's right," he said, though what he was agreeing to or approving of Rachel couldn't have said.

Ambling forward a few steps, he stooped to grasp the steel T-handle of the garage door. Rachel watched the muscles flex beneath his shirt, and then the old door screeched and lifted, revealing his truck. His bright, new, shiny truck. Red, with Massachusetts plates and a bumper sticker that read, Women Love Me, Fish Fear Me.

She shot him a look, trying not to smile.

He grinned. "A present from my sister-in-law. She has a weird sense of humor."

The words popped out before she could censor them. "She must, if your brother's anything like you."

He laughed. "Nah. My brothers are both respectable now."

He climbed into his candy-apple-red truck. Rachel concentrated on negotiating her rental vehicle backward along the gravel, as cautious and awkward as a pregnant woman on roller skates. She felt the soft bump as her rear tire ran on grass and then the firm, flat road.

Sean MacNeill gunned his motor. His galvanized, over-size toolbox gleamed as he reversed toward her at twice her speed and cut smoothly onto the road.

Rachel sighed. She had too much at stake here to risk an attraction to some twenty-something carpenter in tight jeans and a kick-ass truck.

Whatever his motives, Sean MacNeill was a complication she didn't need and a distraction she couldn't afford.

Whatever her mother said, he would have to go.

Chapter 2

Don't be a chump, MacNeill.

Sean punched up the volume on the radio, letting the bass pound away at his frustration. It wasn't his fault Walt Baxley of Baxley Construction was a money-grubbing slimeball. It wasn't Sean's job to bring this project in under budget or up to code. It wasn't his responsibility. But he'd tried, anyway. At least, he'd argued. Definitely chump behavior. Hadn't he learned anything since high school?

Sean wasn't looking to take on unnecessary obligations. The only three things he should apply himself to now were a hot shower, a cold beer and an agreeable woman to...talk with.

He checked his rearview mirror and eased down the gas pedal, betting that the under-manned police department wouldn't ticket him doing sixty-eight on this empty stretch of road. It looked like he already had the second two covered. Lori Tucker, who sold houses for Baxley's seven-million-dollar development, had made it clear she'd be waiting for him at Woody's tonight. Sean liked the real estate agent's style, her neat nails and tumbled hair and tight little power suits. Heck, he liked most women, always had, all ages, shapes and temperaments of women. His sincere appreciation usually compelled their liking in return.

He turned off what passed for the main road, fingers drumming the steering wheel in time to the beat from his custom speakers.

Rachel Fuller had not liked him. Correction. Did not want to like him. Which was going to make sharing a bathroom with her a little tricky.

Pulling into Myra Jordan's driveway, he braked. The rental truck was gone. In its place, blocking his entrance to the garage, stood a haphazard pyramid of moving cartons and a green velvet couch with dragon claws. Curled on the center cushion, the dark-haired little girl with the sulky mouth scowled at the pile. The boy, a paler copy of his sister, perched on the curb, absently bouncing a tennis ball between his feet.

The screen door shrieked. Rachel Fuller appeared on the porch, her glossy hair escaping its ponytail and her face pink with heat and exertion. She was dressed like a soldier in khaki shorts and a plain gray T-shirt. Except no army man ever had thighs like hers.

The day was looking up.

Grinning, Sean got out of the truck.

Rachel stood at the top of the porch steps. "Hey, kiddos. We've got a couple more boxes to move upstairs."

The ball bounced—once, twice—on the hot asphalt. The girl lifted one shoulder and sank deeper into the cushions of the couch.

Sean paused on his way up the driveway. So, her kids

were reluctant to give her a hand. It was none of his business.

"Chris. Lindsey. Come on, now."

The boy stood uncertainly, clutching his tennis ball.

The girl flopped her head back to squint at her mother. "It's too hot," she complained.

Sean saw Rachel sigh. "It is hot. Why don't you come inside and Grandma will get you some lemonade?"

They moved at that, two sets of sandaled feet thumping up the steps, past their mother, for the shaded interior of the house.

Rachel smiled across the yard at Sean. "You want some, too?" she called.

"Sure," he said easily.

He sauntered up the drive. Here it comes, he thought. First the offer of a drink, and then the request for his help. He didn't mind, not really. It wasn't the first time he'd been drafted by Beauty in Distress, and it wouldn't be the last. Okay, so he'd learned to identify the scope of the problem before leaping in, but there was no way Rachel could shift all this stuff with only an elderly woman and two kids to help her. He hitched his thumbs in his pockets and waited.

Rachel stepped off the porch and squared off with a four-foot wardrobe box. She squatted to lift it. With mild offense, he realized that she wasn't going to ask him for help at all.

"Need a hand?"

Her slight smile jabbed his gut like the business end of a two-by-four. She lifted correctly, using those long, smooth legs, and took small steps toward the porch. "I can manage, thanks."

He gestured toward the couch at his feet, a lady's sofa, long and narrow, with velvet cushions and elegant scrolled arms. It looked ridiculous standing in the drive-way.

"What about this?"

She puffed. "What about it?"

He ambled ahead of her to open the door. "Aren't you going to move it in the house?"

"I can't. There's no room."

He looked past her into the shadowed living room. She was right. The front room was already packed with Myra's own big easy pieces. Photographs jammed the mantel and covered the walls. Knick-knacky things decorated every available surface. But, still, it looked pretty good, considering that Rachel must have moved in all her stuff that day. He identified a new little piecrust table, crammed into a corner, and a short stack of boxes waiting to go upstairs.

"Where's the rest?"

She grunted as the cardboard wardrobe slid through her arms and thumped onto the floor. "Up."

Sean thought of the completely furnished bedrooms, the already crowded spare room. "No, I meant your furniture and things."

"There is no furniture. Nothing but the couch."

Sean narrowed his eyes. Myra Jordan, in the way of lonely seniors and mothers everywhere, had bragged to him about her widowed daughter's lovely home in Pennsylvania, her daughter's late, successful husband the car dealer. He'd suspected his new landlady might have a rich fantasy life, but still…why would Rachel Fuller abandon a fully furnished, three-bedroom, two-and-a-half-baths to move across four states and live with her mother?

None of his business, he reminded himself. He had a cold beer and a hot date waiting.

He cleared his throat to make his excuses and leave,

and found himself instead hefting the wardrobe and asking, "Where do you want this?"

"I... My room. But you don't need—"

"I'm on my way up to shower, anyway. Through here?"

"Yes. Thank you."

"No big deal."

No big deal. One box, and he was back to his plans for the evening. He shouldered open the door and stopped dead.

The blue room looked like a warehouse, with cartons everywhere. Sean's own few things—his toiletries and a once-worn pair of jeans, a T-shirt and a picture crayoned by his nephew Jack—were packed and piled in the middle of the neatly made bed. Hell, if these were all Rachel's boxes, no wonder she didn't have room for furniture.

"Maybe I should put this in the kids' room?"

"No," she said firmly. "I'll unpack it in here."

"Whatever." He found a square yard of floor to set the carton down and then gestured toward his kit on the bed. "Mind if I, uh..."

"Please. Everything's there," she added, as if he was going to count his loose change or something.

Scooping up his shaving kit, he made for the shower, brushing by her in the doorway. Not on purpose, not really. Her eyes, the color of oiled mahogany, darkened even further.

He felt the bite of lust and blunted it with a smile. There was no place in his bachelor life for a healthy widow with a matched set of some other man's baggage. "I'll be out of your hair in a minute."

"The children are downstairs. You can change in their room, if you like."

Her big eyes watched him, unconsciously inviting.

Ah, what the hell. He'd never been good at resisting temptation.

"Can I give you a call if I need help? You know, scrubbing my back, buttoning my... No?"

She raised her chin at his teasing. "You look old enough to manage on your own."

"Yeah, that's what my mother said before she kicked me out of the house."

She winced slightly. "Well, then, just think of me as your mother."

"Precocious, were you?"

"Excuse me?"

"Unless you started having babies at five, beautiful, I can't see you as my mother."

She smiled, deepening the creases at the corners of her eyes. "Try again. I'm thirty-four."

"Got it in one. I'm twenty-nine. Do I get to pick my prize?"

Poker-faced, she said, "No, but if you stop now, I might not run the washing machine while you're in the shower."

He laughed, giving her the point, and moseyed down the hall. The door to the spare bedroom stood open.

There were boxes, here, too, two taped cartons on each of the twin beds. But that was all. Her mother's clutter had been hauled out, the evidence of the move tidied away.

Sean stopped in the doorway. Rachel must have slaved all day. Matching blue bedspreads echoed the colors of the lamp and curtains. Books were aligned in the shelves under the window. She'd even hung posters, Sammy Sosa over the boy's bed, a field of flowers over the girl's. She was living in a sea of cardboard, and her kids' room looked like *Decorating on a Budget* in some women's magazine.

God, it took him back. Establishing base camp, Sergeant Major John MacNeill had called it. Sean had a sudden, unsettling memory of the transfer to Beaufort Air Base—or was it Parris Island?—and his mother laughing as she unwrapped six old crayons swathed in tissue and his father hauling boxes from the car.

Who had helped Rachel Fuller? Not that precious pair downstairs, that was obvious.

Oh, hell. Shaking his head, Sean dropped his shaving kit on the toilet seat in the tiny bathroom and went back downstairs.

"Where are you going?" Rachel asked, surprise in her voice.

"To get another box."

There wasn't a lot, he told himself. It was no big deal. If he hustled, he could still be at Woody's by seven. Pretty Lori would wait that long.

At six forty-nine, the pyramid in the driveway was gone, and the pile at the foot of the stairs was gone, and Sean had pulled the kid, Rachel's son, from in front of the TV to help him lug cardboard boxes out to the garbage.

"Hold on." Sean stopped the sullen child before he staggered down the stairs. Pulling out his pocketknife, he slit the tape that held the box together. "You do it like this, and then you can break out the bottom. See?" He demonstrated, folding the carton so that it would stack.

Interest flicked in the boy's closed face. "Cool. Is that yours?"

"Yeah."

"Could I...?"

Sean shrugged. "Sure." Used to brothers, he collapsed

the little knife and offered it to the boy. "You've got to hold it with the blade facing down, okay? Keep your fingers—"

"Oh, no." Rachel Fuller appeared around the bend in the stairs, a tall glass of lemonade sweating in her hand. "Chris, give that back. Now."

The boy dropped the knife as if the metal were red-hot. It bounced once on the edge of the carpet and then slithered across the wood floor to Sean's feet. He scooped it up and returned it to his pocket, smiling up at Rachel's indignant eyes and red cheeks.

"Guess I should have asked."

"I guess you should have." Stiffly, she proffered the lemonade.

He took it, her schoolteacher's tone snapping against his good intentions like a rubber band. So far he'd missed his shower, his dinner and his beer, not to mention an hour of the agreeable Lori Tucker. His loss, Sean figured. His choice. But that didn't mean he had to stick around while Rachel Fuller scowled at him.

He drained the glass, grateful for any cold liquid to hit the back of his throat, and gave it back. "We're almost done, anyway. You want a hand with that couch before I go?"

She wanted to refuse. He could see it in the way she stuck out that pouty lower lip.

And then she ducked her head, her cheeks pinking. "I... Yes, please. It really can't stay outside."

He clomped down the steps behind her. "You should have left it on the truck."

"I would have, but the rental place said I needed to return the truck today." She deposited his empty glass— on a coaster, he noticed, amused by her care—in the living room.

He held the front door open for her, admiring the way she swept through, her tied-up hair bouncing on her shoulders. For all she was so tall and strongly built, she moved nice. Graceful.

He sauntered down the driveway and lifted an end of the silly lady's couch.

"So, where do you want this?"

She looked at him sideways, a hint of challenge in her eyes. "I thought...the garage?"

"Oh, no. Sorry, beautiful. I know better than to let a pretty woman move her stuff into my place."

She set down her end of the sofa. "I think we should get a few things straight. This is not your place. You are renting from my mother. And frankly—"

"Rachel! There you are." Myra Jordan came out onto the porch. "There was a phone call for you, dear. A man."

Just for a moment Sean thought Rachel's shoulders stiffened. And then she bent again easily, arms flexing as she lifted. "Thanks, Mama. Did you take a message?"

"No. No, he didn't leave a message." Myra beamed. "Don't worry, he said he'd call back."

"Did he." Rachel's voice was nearly expressionless, but Sean saw her fingers tighten on the soft plush arm of the couch. "How did he get your number?"

"Well, I... Heavens, I don't know. He said he worked with Doug."

Doug-the-Late-Husband, Sean guessed.

The fingers relaxed a fraction. "Was it Jerry Kline?"

Myra tipped her head to one side. "Kline? No. Actually, I don't think he gave his name."

"But you're sure he worked with Doug? At the dealership?"

"That's what he said. Well, that he was a 'business

associate of your late husband.'" Myra chuckled. "Very formal-sounding, the way he said it."

Rachel's once-flushed face was nearly white. Sean frowned.

Myra's expression creased with concern. "Honey, I'm sorry. I didn't realize you were out here. Are you upset you missed the call? Because he said he'd be in touch."

"No," Rachel said faintly. "No, I'm not upset." She lowered her end of the sofa again and then looked up at Sean. "You stay, the sofa stays."

Her about-face confused him. For a minute there he'd expected her to tell him to get lost. "What?"

The words almost tumbled out. "My mother feels safer having a man around. Maybe she's right. And the couch isn't such a big deal. Think of it as part of a…a furnished lease."

"This couch? Green velvet. In my workshop."

A smile ghosted around her mouth, but her dark eyes never wavered. "It would have to be covered with something, of course."

"Of course," he echoed, amused in spite of himself.

She had some nerve, he'd give her that. He wasn't even sleeping with her, and she already wanted to move in her furniture. Even Trina, in the nine months he thought they were setting up their household— Don't go there, he ordered himself. He didn't want Rachel's sofa. He didn't want to get sucked into her problems, either.

He tugged the hoop in his ear. "Do I get a break in the rent?"

"No." Her quick smile was almost conciliatory. "I don't think one couch requires a lease negotiation, do you? But it would be a place for you to sleep tonight."

"I've got a place to sleep tonight."

"Oh." She looked embarrassed. "I see."

He wasn't explaining Lori Tucker, even assuming the real estate agent had decided to keep his barstool warm. "My brother, Patrick, lives about forty minutes southeast from here. I can grab a bed from him tonight, if I need one, and move in some stuff I need tomorrow."

"That's settled then," she said with evident relief.

But nothing was really settled, Rachel thought later, listening to the truck's engine rev away into the warm, soft twilight. Nothing was settled at all. Guilt clutched at her. If she hadn't been late with that one payment... If she'd been a better wife to Doug... If she'd gone to the police in the first place...

Rachel shivered. No. She couldn't do that. Carmine Bilotti had made the danger of contacting the police very clear.

And so Rachel found herself agreeing to let Sean MacNeill stay, as if his presence in the garage could somehow deter the bad guys. But she wondered uneasily if the tall young carpenter, with his pirate looks and his wicked smile and his air of lazy challenge, wasn't danger of another kind.

"I'm so glad you changed your mind about Sean, dear," Myra said, popping open the oven door to check on the meat loaf. Heat rolled out into the kitchen. "Are you sure he couldn't stay for dinner?"

"He had plans. And I didn't really change my mind, Mama. I mean, it's your house. Your decision. I hardly know him."

"Well, you're going to like him once you get to know him," Myra declared. She lifted a pot lid, poked at the greens inside. "He's a nice young man."

"Too young."

"Twenty-nine."

"So he told me."

Myra smiled with satisfaction. "There, you see? You're getting to know each other already."

"Mama, you're not thinking…" Rachel sighed. She knew exactly what her mother was thinking. Myra Jordan believed human beings should walk paired, like animals on the Ark. Once Rachel had thought so, too. Before Doug's deception had shattered her world and her trust and left her alone, yoked to her obligations.

"Forget it, Mama," she said.

"Why?"

"I'm not looking for a relationship right now." Ever, she amended silently.

"Honey, Douglas died a year ago. Is it so wrong for me to want to see my only daughter happy?"

Rachel rattled open the silverware drawer. "Douglas died in *debt*, Mama. I'm still dealing with that."

"But things will be better now that you've sold the house."

Rachel wished. She tightened her grip on the forks. "Not really. Most of that money had to go back into the business."

Myra's eyes widened. "The dealership? Why?"

Rachel hesitated, reluctant to dump her load of worry on her mother. To feed his gambling habit, Doug had "borrowed" thousands of dollars from his business. Once she'd accepted executorship, Rachel had taken it upon herself to pay her late husband's debts. *All* his debts. Some she paid because it was her legal and moral responsibility. And some she paid from fear.

"Some sort of claim against the estate," she answered vaguely. "Anyway, it's cheaper to live down here. And once I start teaching, we can look for an apartment."

"If that's what you want..." her mother said doubtfully.

It was what she had. "All I want is some security. Some stability. The children have had enough changes in the past year."

"What about you? Heavens, Rachel, you didn't used to be such a—well, such a stick. You used to climb trees and talk back to your teachers and drive that little car of yours too fast. Maybe I complained you were giving me gray hair, but at least you used to be able to have a little fun. Take a few chances."

Rachel shivered, remembering. *Take a chance,* Doug used to urge her, his blue eyes alight. *Live a little.* Until his own compulsive risk-taking had bankrupted their future and driven him to his death.

She shrugged the memories away. "I guess I grew up."

"Nonsense. You're still a young woman. What about fun?"

"I don't have fun," she said harshly. Too harshly, she recognized. "I have responsibilities."

"What about love?"

The question hurt like a finger poked in an unhealed wound. Rachel drew a shaky breath. But she put down the flowered plates she remembered from her childhood and walked around the dark pine table and put her arms around Myra's shoulders. Even barefoot, she was a full head taller than her mother.

"I love you, Mama. I love Lindsey, and I love Chris. And that's all the love I need. All I can handle."

The wall phone shrilled. Rachel stiffened. Oblivious to her tension, her mother bustled across the kitchen to answer it. She listened a moment.

"It's for you, dear." Beaming, Myra covered the receiver with her hand and whispered, "I told you he'd call back."

Chapter 3

"**D**id the caller threaten you, Miz Fuller? Or your children?"

Sean stopped dead in the hall, his right hand curling as if it held a hammer. He wasn't involved, he reminded himself. He wasn't getting involved. But even without the black-and-white police cruiser pulled up in front of the house, he would have made the speaker as a cop.

Rachel's voice, stretched tight as a coping saw wire, carried from the kitchen. "No. Nothing like that. I told you, it was nothing."

"Your mother said you were agitated."

"Agitated? No. Well, I mean... I shouldn't have been. I'm a teacher. New in town. It was probably just some kids, playing a prank."

"Miz Jordan said the caller was a man. With a northern accent, she said."

"I guess."

"And you're from Pennsylvania."

"That's right."

"Did you recognize the caller?"

Her voice jumped. "No!"

Sean, listening in the hall, thought she made a lousy liar. He felt a familiar protective surge in his gut: the same damn chivalrous impulse that had driven him in kindergarten to defend five-year-old Jenny Lopez's honor, the guy-in-the-white-hat routine responsible for most of the trouble and half the relationships he'd stumbled into in the past twenty years.

Don't be a chump, he reminded himself. So, Rachel Fuller didn't want the police to know she had a secret admirer. Her decision. Her problem.

"Any idea how he got hold of your mother's number?"

"She's in the phone book. Listen, Officer, I know she made it sound like I'd been attacked or something. And I was a little upset. But I'm fine now."

"Yes, ma'am. You let us know if the problem persists, and we can put you in touch with the phone company's annoyance call center. They can trace the calls if..."

An accusing whisper shot from the top of the stairs. "What are you doing here?"

Sean tipped his head back. Rachel's dark-haired daughter crouched halfway down the first flight, her elbows on her knees and her pointed chin in her hands. She had her mother's mouth, he thought. Full and stubborn.

"Eavesdropping," Sean said. "Same as you, I guess. You okay?"

She sniffed. "I'm fine. Grandma's making a fuss because some man called Mom again."

Sean frowned. Again?

"You think?" he asked easily. "You listen in on the phone call, too?"

She glared at him.

And like a boxer too dumb to skip town at the sound of the bell, Sean winked at her and ambled into the kitchen.

"Hi, honey, I'm home."

Rachel straightened in her chair. Sean's breezy entrance lightened the heated atmosphere like an unexpected gust on a sweltering day. The man was outrageous. Intrusive. Welcome.

Facing her across the kitchen table, Officer Gary Miller sat to attention. Rachel knew the patrolman slightly. Well, she remembered his brother. They'd taken American History together in high school. The police officer had the same baby face imperfectly concealed by a bristly brown mustache, the same wrestler's body, the same stiff, light brown hair. The badge was new, and the gun at his hip, and the nightstick-up-his-back attitude.

"Who is this?" he asked.

Sean strolled forward. Rachel watched as the patrolman took in the disreputable jeans, the movie star stubble and the earring.

"Sean MacNeill. I live here," he added.

A slight flush crawled under the officer's tan. "Do you mean you, uh…"

It was almost funny. Rachel felt as if they were back in high school and the young policeman was deciding whether or not to scrawl her phone number on his gym locker. *For a good time call…*

"Sean rents the garage from my mother," she explained.

Miller made a note. "New to these parts, Mr. Mac-Neill?"

"You could say so. I've been working construction in the Triangle the last couple of years."

"Where are you from originally?"

"Boston."

"And where were you last night around..." The policeman consulted his notebook. "Seven-thirty?"

Sean leaned one hip against the counter, crossed his arms over his chest. "Out."

Oh, for heaven's sake, Rachel thought. She couldn't afford to have the police questioning her about her mystery caller. But she couldn't let them suspect Sean, either. "It wasn't him. The first call came when he was helping me move in."

Sean looked at her, brown eyes steady. "What's this all about, anyway?"

Miller tapped his pen against his notebook. "Miz Fuller received an annoying phone call. I asked her for the names of possible suspects."

"And that would be me," Sean guessed, an indefinable edge to his voice.

"I never said you did it," Rachel said quickly.

The officer shrugged. "New to the area. Northern accent. It was worth checking out."

Sean raised an eyebrow, looking like every woman's bad boy fantasy. "What, exactly, haven't I done?"

Rachel hesitated. Carmine Bilotti had made it clear she wasn't beyond his reach yet. She should warn Sean, tell him...what? She couldn't say anything with the policeman there ready to jot down every word.

She shook her head. "Like the officer said, I got some unpleasant phone calls. Mother called to report them, and I'm taking care of it. We don't need your help."

"Well, that's a relief."

He pushed away from the counter. This time his smile didn't reach his eyes. "You know where to find me if you change your mind. Or if Officer Friendly here needs me for questioning."

She watched him go, his stride easy and his shoulders tight, and an unaccustomed regret echoed inside her like footsteps in an empty classroom. Something in Sean MacNeill's pose of concern, the strength implicit in his wrists and his voice, pulled at her.

She sighed. Right. Like he could do something for her. Like she had anything to offer him. She was a widow in debt to small-time criminals, struggling to provide for two children and living with her mother. She would handle this the way she'd learned to handle everything else.

Alone.

It *was* a relief, Sean thought, to get back to the simple, physical chore of unloading his truck. He'd always found peace in things he could touch, things he could mold, things that yielded to sweat and labor. Good with his hands, his cousin Ross the builder had said, and scores of former girlfriends could attest that it was true.

He pulled the canvas back from the sides of the truck. He'd only brought a few pieces from his brother's barn along on this trip: a chimney cupboard, the skeleton of a desk, several variations of a—side table? night table?— he was just about satisfied with. But the simple, elegant pieces appeased some ache inside him that all his amiable liaisons hadn't touched.

"Wow. You have a lot of furniture."

At the sound of the child's voice, he turned. It was the boy, he saw. Chris. About his nephew Jack's age but smaller, with short brown hair and hazel eyes and his mother's cautious expression.

Sean smiled, to show he wouldn't bite, and dropped the tailgate. "It's not all mine," he said, spreading the quilted padding to protect the red paint, the unfinished wood.

"The cupboard's for my sister-in-law, and two of those tables are going to a shop."

"What for?"

"To sell."

The boy nodded. "We sold our furniture. Lindsey was mad, and Mom cried."

Sean grunted. He didn't want to know, didn't want to picture those soldier's shoulders defeated, that full mouth thinned with grief. He lifted a table from the back of the truck, careful to keep the tapered legs clear of the sides. Why had she sold their furniture?

We don't need your help.

"Can I help you?" Chris asked suddenly.

Sean set the table down and gripped the handle of the garage door. "Shouldn't you be giving your mom a hand?"

The boy looked down and away. "She's busy."

With the police. Although as far as Sean could tell, Rachel Fuller was always busy. The pity was that beyond the slight support of her mother, he couldn't see that she had anyone to help her. Not that he was applying for the job. He wasn't that big a chump.

He hauled on the door and then stopped with his arms extended above his head. Something was different.

Over the past week he'd put in several sixteen-hour days hauling trash, scrubbing and sealing the walls and the floor, installing lights, shelves and fixtures. His planned living area in the loft would have to wait until he rigged the plumbing from the mud sink below. But along the back wall where he'd cleared a space for his larger pieces, somebody had somehow maneuvered the fancy dragon-claw sofa. Two pillows and a folded quilt rested on the cushions.

He glanced over his shoulder at the boy. "You do this?"

Chris shifted from foot to foot, uncertain with attention. "Mom did. But I helped."

So, Rachel Fuller had been busy again. On his behalf, this time.

"Well." Green velvet. He grinned. What in hell was he supposed to do with green velvet? "It looks good. Thanks."

The boy bobbed his head. He stood there, not really in the way, not ever out of sight, while Sean unloaded two tables and a cot.

It was probably pretty lousy moving to a new town right before the start of the school year. Frowning, Sean went back for the chimney cupboard. The boy slid out of his way.

Hell. Chris Fuller's social life was none of his business. Sean needed to unload the truck and haul butt back to work. Walt Baxley, still stewing over yesterday's argument over load calculations, had only grudgingly granted him the morning off. Being late would really tick him off.

The police officer came out of the house and down the steps. With a nod to Sean, he backed up his weather-beaten cruiser and drove away.

Sean angled the cupboard to avoid the overhang, taking small careful steps, watching the roof.

"Look out!" the boy said suddenly.

Sean stopped.

Chris darted forward, crouched, and then stood, dragging away a fold of packing cloth. "You were going to trip."

"Thanks."

Sean grunted, lifting the lathe.

The kid didn't go away. "What is that?"

"Heavy?" Sean suggested. His nephew would have cracked up at the feeble joke. Chris merely watched him with those too solemn hazel eyes. "A lathe," he said. "It's a lathe."

"What does it do?"

"Turns and carves things. Table legs, stuff like that." The boy nodded.

Sean set the lathe along the garage wall. He had a sudden memory of Patrick, kinglike in his generosity, and Con, smiling with amused tolerance, heading out for a game of catch, for sodas at the corner drugstore, for a Friday night cruise in Patrick's car. It didn't matter what, as long as they were out and together. *Sure, buddy, you can come along.*

He sighed. "Hey, sport, I could use a hand here."

Bingo. The sport's smile switched on like a utility lamp.

"Sure," he said.

Rachel pushed open the screen door, blinking against the flood of sunshine that slanted under the eaves of the porch and poured over the driveway. A dark blot formed in the center of the brightness, taking on shape and substance and power. A man's shape, she identified a moment later, lifting something—a box—from the back of a truck. Sean MacNeill, in a T-shirt with the arms ripped out and a faded baseball cap, moving like Apollo in the heart of fire.

Her knees, her spine and her jaw all sagged. She caught herself reacting to him for a moment purely as woman to man, warmed by the glow of his tall, dark and blatantly sexy good looks. It was totally involuntary. It was... stupid, she reminded herself.

Doug's death had trapped her in a high-stakes game

with uncertain rules and her children's future on the table. A joker like Sean MacNeill wouldn't help her odds at all. But, goodness, he was gorgeous to watch.

He saw her. Setting down the box, he straightened, pushing back the brim of his cap with his forearm. His slow smile thumped into her midsection and quivered like an arrow.

"Hey, beautiful."

"Oh, please." She flapped her hand. "You can call me Rachel."

"Rachel." He lingered wickedly over the name, rolling it in his mouth like something delicious. "Well, it suits you. But then, so does 'beautiful.'"

She was amused. "Me, and everyone else you know?"

He came up to the porch, all long bones and male muscle, and tipped back his head to look at her. Her heart actually fluttered. "How do you figure that?" he asked.

"Well, for a man who must spend his time in the company of a lot of women, 'beautiful' is convenient. I mean, it saves you the trouble of remembering who you're... with."

He grinned. "So?"

"So, since it's unlikely I'll ever be offended by your whispering some other woman's name in my ear, you can just use 'Rachel.'" She smiled back at him, pleased by her own composure.

"If I promise to remember who I'm kissing, can I still call you beautiful?"

She flushed. "I don't think it's going to be an issue." She glanced over his head toward the driveway. "Have you seen Chris? My son?"

"Yeah, he's around." He pitched his voice toward the garage. "Hey, sport! Your mom's here. I put him to work unpacking boxes," he explained.

"You did?"

"You got a problem with that? Going to report me to Officer Friendly for violating child labor laws?"

"No. Oh, no. I'm just wondering how you got him to help."

He leaned against the railing, exuding heat and sex appeal. She could see the damp hair curling under the plastic band at the back of his cap and the sweat darkening his T-shirt. "He was underfoot anyway. I asked."

She stiffened at the implicit criticism. "I apologize if he was in your way."

He shrugged. "'S okay. I worked around him."

"The children are going through a very difficult time right now."

"Sounds like you are, too."

His observation surprised her. She didn't expect a twenty-something bachelor to understand her children's claims or her own fears. "I manage," she said lightly.

He hesitated; opened his mouth as if he might say something, but then Chris came out of the garage.

"I got your books lined up like you told me," he announced.

"Great," Sean said.

The schoolteacher in Rachel wondered what kind of reading material would appeal to a man who wore a T-shirt proclaiming Beauty is in the Eye of the Beer Holder. Science fiction? How-to manuals?

"What sort of books?" she asked.

He shot her a look through thick, dark lashes. "Anything I can read without moving my lips." He raised his voice to reach Chris. "Did you want to borrow that Calvin and Hobbes?"

Comic books. Her little sting of embarrassment faded away. Of course.

Chris shuffled his feet. "I guess. Sure."

"Say thank you," Rachel prompted.

"Thanks, Mr. MacNeill."

"Any time, sport."

The boy darted into the garage.

Sean angled his cap back on his head. "It's none of my business, but it seems to me both your kids could probably use more to do."

Guilt bit her. "I know. School starts next week, and all their friends are back in Pennsylvania. I'd hoped to take them around more, to the library, to the movies, but I still have lesson plans to prepare. And with the move…"

"I meant, they could give you more of a hand."

"I don't really think you're in a position to judge."

"Maybe not. I have brothers."

"But no children."

A muscle in his jaw ticked. "Nope." And then he turned his head, speculation gleaming in his eyes. "You want to ask me about my love life now?"

"I'm sure it's fascinating," she said, trying for cool.

"Not really."

"Then there's no one…special?" Not cool, she realized instantly. Not cool at all. She might as well come right out and ask if he was sleeping with anyone.

"I didn't say that. There are four very special ladies in my life."

She tried not to goggle. "Four?"

"Mmm. Only one of them's after me to get married, though."

"Oh?"

"Yeah. *She* thinks I'd make a great father."

She pursed her mouth. "Really."

"The way she sees it, I have an obligation to share my gene pool."

She looked at him sideways, unsure if he were joking. "That's the most ridiculous thing I ever heard."

"I don't know about ridiculous. A little over-the-top, maybe, but, hey, a guy's mother is bound to be partial."

She narrowed her eyes at him. "Your mother."

He grinned like an unrepentant dog. "Yeah."

Her breath blew out in a quick laugh. "I've been had, haven't I? Who are the other three women? Your sisters?"

"Two sisters-in-law. And my niece, Brianna. She's two."

So he was someone's "uncle" after all. "A real family man," Rachel said.

He looked away, across the drive. "Not really. I don't mind kids, if that's what you're asking. But I'm not looking to take on someone else's family."

She didn't know whether to be offended or amused. "You sound like you're answering a Personals ad."

"Do I?" His dark gaze returned to her face. "Are you advertising, Rachel?"

Quick heat washed her cheeks. "No."

"Hey, we're going to be living pretty close for a while. I'm attracted. It's only reasonable to put our cards on the table."

"Look, I don't know what my mother's told you, but—"

"Only that it's been over a year since you lost your husband."

"Did she also tell you he killed himself?"

There was no faking his shock. No disguising it, either. She smiled without any joy and with a thin satisfaction that made her ashamed.

"It was a surprise to me, too," she said.

"I didn't know. Sorry for your loss."

Once again his consideration disarmed her. "Thank

you." Painfully she added, "I'm sorry, too. I don't usually bludgeon strangers with that one."

"It's understandable. You're dealing with this move. Some jerk is hassling you on the phone. And you just had the police for breakfast. That's enough to rattle anybody."

"Yes."

She was more than rattled. She was scared. *I'm sorry about the house, Mrs. Fuller,* Bilotti had explained with seeming regret. *My nephew, Frank, he gets carried away sometimes. But you got to understand we can't let you run out on this deal. It wouldn't be good for business.*

She swallowed. "I only wanted to make it clear this isn't a good time…I'm not in the market for a man or a relationship right now."

Sean was silent so long she wondered queasily if she'd just made a total fool of herself.

"Of course I know you were only teasing," she added.

He took off his cap and studied the inside, as if the answer to some exam question were secreted in the brim. "I didn't figure you for a woman without responsibilities. And, yeah, I generally limit myself to the other kind. But I'm not kidding myself, beautiful, and I won't kid you, either." The gold hoop gleamed as he turned his head. His lazy smile caught her right under the rib cage, stealing her breath. "When I said I was attracted, I wasn't teasing."

Chapter 4

"I'm not moving them." Crossing her arms against her chest, Lindsey glared at her mother, obviously ready to go to the wall and die before she'd touch a single stuffed animal. "I just got them all arranged."

Rachel's heart constricted. She sympathized with her daughter's desperate determination to organize the mess life had handed them. But she held firm.

"Three shelves each, Lindsey. That's what we agreed."

"But Chris doesn't need that shelf. He said I could have it."

To keep the peace, Chris would agree to almost anything. Rachel sighed. She knew the feeling. "That was very nice of him. But he will need it when school starts."

"So?"

"So, you have to share."

Lindsey's lower lip protruded. "I didn't have to share at home. I want my old room back."

"I know it's difficult, honey, but—"

"I miss our house. I miss my friends."

She missed her daddy, Rachel thought with another squeeze of heart. Lindsey had always been more like her father than her mother: impulsive, spontaneous, charming.

Irresponsible.

Rachel pushed the thought away. Kneeling on the floor in front of the bookcase, she reached to smooth her daughter's tumbled hair. "You'll make new friends."

"I wish we never moved here," Lindsey muttered.

"Well, we're here now, and we have to make the best of it. Why don't you and Chris try setting up the shelves together?"

"He's not here."

Rachel swallowed her alarm. *Don't overreact.* "Where is he?"

"Outside. I think he was looking for that MacNeill guy."

"Mr. MacNeill," Rachel corrected automatically.

Lindsey rolled her eyes. "Whatever."

Rachel sat back on her heels. It was just her luck that Chris would seek out Sean MacNeill when she was doing her darnedest to avoid the man. Every time she turned around, he was barreling in and out of the driveway in his shiny red truck. Sauntering in and out of the bathroom in clouds of steam and pheromones. Slipping in and out of her awareness with his loose-limbed stride and easy grin.

She hadn't felt this attuned to a man's presence since the summer she turned twelve and fourteen-year-old Hank Simmons rode his ten-speed past the bottom of her driveway.

"Your face is all red," Lindsey said.

Rachel felt her blush deepen. "It's hot in here." She

climbed to her feet. "I'm going to get your brother. See if you can work something out, okay?"

Lindsey ducked her head. "Okay."

Somewhere inside the misery, a very nice child struggled to get out. Rachel dropped a kiss on her hair before she went downstairs.

She'd probably find Chris hanging around the garage. Around Sean. Anticipation licked along Rachel's veins. Stupid, she chided herself. She knew better than to gamble on Tall, Dark and Unreliable.

And if she were ever tempted to forget the lessons of her marriage, she had the sick flutter in her chest every time the phone rang to remind her.

But before she even crossed the kitchen, the back door opened and Chris scuttled inside.

"Where are you going, honey?"

He stopped. Reluctantly, she thought. "Upstairs."

"You want to help your sister organize your shelves?"

"Okay."

Rachel narrowed her eyes at his quick compliance. "Just what were you do—"

The back door rattled under an impatient knock. They both jumped. Heart pounding, Rachel peered through the screen. A man loomed in the shadows of the porch. A large, dark man. Sean MacNeill.

Her heart didn't slow at all.

He looked hot and grim, his usual grin missing. Concern welled inside her. Chris bolted for the stairs.

And Myra came through the living room arch wearing blue house slippers and a wide smile. "Why, Sean! You're home early."

She opened the door. Rachel watched Sean readjust his expression to something pleasant, the forced transformation reminding her uncomfortably of Doug. What was wrong? What was he hiding?

He nodded. "Mrs. Jordan."

"Did you just get off work? You must be hot. Can I get you something to drink? Tea?"

"No. No, thanks. I wonder if I could talk to your daughter a minute."

"Of course." She beamed at them both.

Oh, Mama. "Alone, I think he means, Mama," Rachel said.

He leveled a look at her from under dark eyebrows. "I don't want to throw your mother out of her own kitchen. Why don't you come outside? I've got something you ought to see in the garage."

Worry skittered along her nerves like a mouse let loose in a classroom. She wouldn't let him intimidate her. At least, she wouldn't let him see that he intimidated her.

Slowly, she moved toward the door. "All right."

"Is this a variation on going out to the woodshed?" she quipped as they crossed the backyard.

"Could be. You going to let me spank you?"

She stopped dead in the dusty grass, appalled. Excited, for heaven's sake. "Certainly not."

He shrugged. "Okay. I didn't think you did it, anyway."

"Did what? What are you talking about?"

Sean admired the snooty schoolteacher tone after the quick sparkle of excitement he'd seen in her eyes. The combination was unexpectedly appealing. She was something, Rachel Fuller.

He reached in front of her to open the small side door, the door he'd repaired two days ago and hadn't seen the need to lock. "In here."

She marched past him like a building inspector on a

power trip and then stopped in the middle of the painted floor. Her eyes widened. He watched her take in the clean white walls, the swept gray floor, the sunshine that dropped through the newly installed skylights. Sawdust glimmered in the air around her, stirred by a lazy fan. She turned slowly, her gaze traveling over the massive workbench to the ordered rows of handsaws and hammers and chisels. Her look stroked over the unpainted cabinet and lingered on the skeleton of a desk.

"Oo-hh," she said, a long note of discovery and pleasure. Pride pulsed in Sean's chest; and then those wide dark eyes turned to him, and he watched her guard go back up.

"It looks very nice. Is that what you want me to say?"

His hunger for her approval annoyed him. He pushed up the bill of his cap with one hand. "I don't give a damn if you like it or not. I brought you here to see the rocker."

"The...?" She turned where he pointed.

His latest project, a Windsor-inspired chair, balanced on tapered legs. He'd worked like a son of a bitch to get the grain flowing through and along every curve, shaping the seat so perfectly with the body grinder it looked like an impression in wet sand.

Except there, across one cheek, where the harsh disc edge had skidded, gouging the surface, destroying the line. The discarded grinder lay on the floor beside the chair.

Rachel frowned. "I don't understand."

"Somebody came in while I was at work today and took the tool to that chair. I doubt it was you, and it sure as hell wasn't your mother."

"You think one of my children..."

"I think Chris did it, yeah. He was in here yesterday while I was sweeping with the grinder."

Her shoulders braced. "How bad is it?"

Sean ran his hand over the contour, feeling the gouge in the wood as if it were a scar in his own skin. "It'll take time to fix. If it can be fixed at all."

"I am so sorry. I'll talk to Chris. He'll apologize."

"That's not going to fix the damage. This is good redwood."

She flushed. "I'll pay for it, of course."

"It's not the money. The kid shouldn't have been in here at all."

Her head snapped back as if he'd slapped her. "I know that. I do apologize. I can assure you there's no question of liability."

He looked at her in disbelief. "You're not going to sue, so I should feel better?"

"I know it wasn't your fault. I should have supervised Chris more closely."

She sounded as guilty as a five-year-old making her first confession. Never mind his ruined work, wasted time and invaded space; he felt kind of bad for her.

"Let me talk to him."

She blinked. "Chris? Why?"

He wasn't sure. It wasn't his kid. It wasn't his problem. But it was his chair, he rationalized. And his complaint. She shouldn't have to deal with it alone, the way she wrestled with everything else.

"Well, for starters, he could explain what he was doing in here."

"I'll talk with him."

"Fine. But I still want my explanation."

Rachel looked him straight in the eye. "After I talk to him."

His mother would have approved of her protective attitude. Bridget had been fierce in her own sons' defense.

Even when they hadn't deserved it. He grinned a little, remembering. Maybe, in his case, especially when he hadn't deserved it.

He hitched his thumbs in his belt loops. "All right. I'll wait."

She studied him a moment, her generous mouth unsure. And then she nodded. "I'll be back in a minute."

A minute. He could stay mad that long. There were things he needed to say, things the kid needed to hear. But it was hard to remember them as Rachel walked away, the sun gleaming on her glossy dark hair, the muscles flexing in her captain-of-the-girls'-soccer-team thighs. The sensible hem of her shorts revealed a band of paler skin. He wanted to run his tongue over it.

He looked away. *Don't be a chump, MacNeill.*

Rachel looked nearly as miserable as her son as they walked back across the parched grass, leaving silver footprints behind them. The kid looked up at Sean, hazel eyes wide in his white face, and then down.

Making Sean feel like Darth Flipping Vader about to order the destruction of the planet. Hell.

Rachel's hand tightened briefly on her son's shoulder, in warning or support. "Go ahead, Chris."

"I'm sorry, Mr. MacNeill," the kid mumbled to his shoes. "I shouldn't have come into the garage."

Rachel sighed. "And?"

The boy's dark head sank even lower between his bony shoulders. "And I shouldn't have touched anything, and I won't do it again."

"You want to tell me what you thought you were doing?" Sean asked.

"I saw you... Yesterday, you were... I wanted to help," he said.

Sean squashed a surge of sympathy. How many times, as a boy, had he used that excuse himself? "Didn't work out that way, though, did it?"

Rachel stirred. "He didn't mean to—"

"Oh, I know. Good intentions, right? They've gotten me in trouble, too. Or hurt. What if I'd been using the chain saw yesterday afternoon? Would you have 'helped' with that?"

The kid looked glum. That was all right. That was good. Rachel looked sick. Not so good.

Sean cleared his throat. "You got to ask permission, sport. Before you touch *anything*. Is that clear?"

The boy nodded.

"You don't need to worry," Rachel said. "Chris is not allowed in the garage again."

Sean had been about to suggest something like that himself. Tools and kids... Hadn't he and Patrick decided his workshop should be off-limits to Jack? But Rachel's staunch acceptance of responsibility, instead of letting him off the hook, made him feel guilty.

"It's okay," he heard himself say. "The kid doesn't bother me. As long as I'm around, he can—"

"No. I appreciate the offer, but watching over my son is not your job."

"If he's going to mess around with tools, he ought to learn to do it safely."

"Chris's safety is my responsibility. And I don't want him 'messing around with tools.'"

Her persistent refusal of help—his help—was beginning to tick him off.

"Listen, I can lock my doors, but you can't lock the kid up. If he wants to get out of the henhouse once in a while..."

"Excuse me?" Her voice took on the edge of a chip-carving knife.

Drop it, MacNeill. After the disaster with Trina in his senior year of high school, he'd promised himself no more Mr. Family Man. He wasn't making points with the woman by volunteering to baby-sit, anyway.

But he opened his big fat mouth and said, "Kid's living with his mom, his grandma and his sister. Let him come out and do the guy thing once in a while."

"Playing with power tools?" she asked dryly.

He gestured toward the chair. "It wouldn't be the first time. Better if he learns how from me."

"Thank you. I'm sure you mean well, but..."

The doubt in her voice woke too damn many echoes from his past.

"But what?"

"You obviously have no experience at being a parent."

Only three months she couldn't know about. The reminder burned like turpentine in a cut. "Yeah, well, I had plenty at being a boy. At least my way he doesn't get hurt and he doesn't gouge a fifty-four-dollar piece of redwood."

"I told you I would pay for that."

"I'll send you a bill. In the meantime, what about teaching Chris a little responsibility?"

Wild color flooded her face. Her knuckles whitened on the boy's shoulders, making him squirm.

Sean felt like a jerk.

And then she drilled right through him with her cool, low voice, each word sharp and perfectly enunciated.

"I've spent the past year learning all about responsibility, Mr. MacNeill. I can teach my son responsibility. But if I thought he needed more lessons, the last person I'd send him to would be someone like you."

* * *

Myra eased into the chair opposite her daughter with a sigh. "We haven't seen much of Sean this week. You two didn't have words, did you?"

Worse than words. Rachel buried her nose and her guilt in the cutting board. She'd been rude. But then, Sean MacNeill had rattled her with his knowing dark eyes and his unexpected offer of help and his unwelcome accusation of irresponsibility.

Irresponsible? Rachel swept her perfectly squared French fries into a stainless-steel bowl. She'd never been irresponsible in her life.

But he tempted her to it. Oh, he tempted her.

"I don't know what you mean by 'words,' Mama. We said 'hello' outside the bathroom this morning."

Myra perked up. "And?"

"And nothing."

If you didn't count the moment of tension when Sean came out of the shower with his clean wet hair and pirate stubble and bland, dismissive smile. She fumbled with the plastic wrap, remembering.

"I think he's having trouble at that job of his," Myra volunteered.

"How would you know?"

"A woman can always tell."

"Not always," Rachel said rashly.

Myra's soft face creased with concentration. "Honey...was there some problem with Doug you never told me about?"

Yes.

"No, Mama. Of course not. Should I make a salad?"

Myra sighed, disappointed of her gossip. "You're always so...practical, dear," she said.

The accusation in her voice made Rachel wince. She

got up to turn on the broiler, ignoring the heat it would add to the already stifling kitchen.

"Mrs. Jordan? Have you got a minute?"

Sean's voice, clear and confident. Bent over the stove, Rachel sucked in a ragged breath. He stomped into the kitchen in boots, smelling of sun and clay and man and looking like some construction worker fantasy on a Hunk-of-the-Month calendar. He wore sweat as if a photographer's assistant had applied it with a spray bottle, and a battered blue cap that read Sure, Work Pays Off—But Laziness Pays Off Now.

She backed defensively into the counter and crossed her arms.

"Love the hat," she drawled.

"Thanks." He took it off. His hair was tied back in a stubby ponytail, dulled with dust.

Myra smiled. "Here for dinner? Rachel's making wonderful cheeseburgers."

She ducked her head, embarrassed by her mother's plug of her domestic skills. "School starts Monday," she explained. "I'm cooking all the children's favorites."

He barely glanced at her, his eyes glittering like Doug's after a high-stakes game. The air around him shimmered with suppressed... Temper? Excitement? Her own adrenaline level rocketed in response. "I almost never say no to food. But actually I came to give your mother the receipts."

He slid a battered clipboard across the dark pine table.

Myra fluttered, rising from her chair without taking it. Without even looking at it. "Oh, yes. Of course. Let me get my checkbook."

The word "checkbook" rang like the five-minute warning bell that signaled the start of school. Rachel cleared her throat. "What receipts?"

When Myra didn't answer, Sean shrugged and replied, "For building supplies."

"Home repair?" Rachel asked.

"Renovating the garage."

The warning bell turned into a siren. "My mother's paying for your workshop?"

"Your mother's paying for improvements to her property. I'm paying for my workshop."

A little demon of doubt prompted her forward. She twisted the clipboard around. He'd printed a neat list on a yellow pad, like one of her own lesson plans, and stapled a slim sheaf of receipts behind. She scanned them quickly. Paint. Pipes. Drywall. She saw charges for the fan and for the door lock. She didn't find any listings for power tools or skylights or fifty-four-dollar pieces of redwood. Some of the tension left her stomach.

Myra retrieved her pocketbook from the utility cart by the door. "I thought it would be nice to have a—what did you call it, Sean?"

"A mother-in-law apartment," he said, his gaze steady on Rachel's face. She felt the hot blood crawl into her cheeks.

"Yes, a mother-in-law apartment over the garage. He said it could be a source of income for me."

Maybe. "Income?" Rachel asked. "You mean, your rent?"

He hesitated. "Actually, that's the other thing I need to discuss with you, Mrs. Jordan."

Myra paused with her pen extended over her posy-pink checks.

Here it comes, Rachel thought. Another man wanted to take advantage. She could hardly object to Sean's living rent-free at Myra Jordan's expense—wasn't she doing the same?—but disappointment pinched her. She'd actually hoped this one was on the level.

"I'd like you to accept my labor on this project in lieu of rent, at least until the end of next week," Sean said evenly.

Myra blinked. "Well, I guess that would be…"

Different, Rachel thought. None of the "uncles" had ever suggested they work for their bed and board.

"Why?" she asked.

He hitched his thumbs in his belt loops. "One, because it's a fair return for my time. And, two, because as of today I'm officially unemployed."

"Oh, dear," Myra said.

Rachel bit back her instinctive sympathy. Someone had to look out for her mother. Someone *responsible*. "I'm sorry. Fired?"

He laughed shortly. "No. Quit."

"Why?" she asked again.

"What is it with you? Do you stop and gawk at traffic accidents, too? Poke the victims?"

She winced, but her voice was cool and steady. "I want to know. And if you're asking for an accommodation in your rent, I think my mother has the right to know."

"Rachel, dear, I really don't need—"

"It's okay, Mrs. Jordan. She's got a point. And I don't figure either one of you is going to report back to Walt Baxley and get me sued for libel."

"Baxley? Is he your boss?"

"He was. Baxley Construction. 'Fine homes at affordable prices.' Or shoddy ones at rip-off rates, but that's my opinion."

"Is that why you quit?"

"I quit because to cheat the building code Old Walt needed a hired monkey, not a carpenter."

Myra clasped her hands together. "How principled of you," she said approvingly.

Reluctant admiration moved in Rachel. "Integrity is good," she said. "But what will you live on?"

"Not your mother, if that's what has your shorts in a twist." He grinned at her the way Doug used to, back in the days when her good opinion still meant something to him. "Something will turn up."

She'd heard that before, too. The easy way he made light of her concerns drove her nuts. "Did you get a reference?"

Myra protested. "Rachel, really…"

"I don't need Baxley's recommendation. I'm not saying the phone's going to ring off the wall with offers, but—"

The phone did ring, reverberating in the heated atmosphere. Sean laughed, surprised and quick.

Rachel fought the insidious warm-and-fuzzy effect of his laughter. Why was she the only one who saw the seriousness of the situation? She was tired of trying to protect her mother from unsuitable men. She was tired of fighting her own attraction to a laid-back, out-of-work, twenty-something carpenter. And she was sick to death of worrying about money.

She snatched the receiver off the wall. "Hello?"

"Mrs. Fuller?"

Her heart stopped at the sound of that heavy, solicitous voice. "I thought you weren't going to call me here anymore."

"Did I say that?" He sounded genuinely surprised. "No, I wouldn't want you to think I'd forgotten about you down there. I got the last check in the mail, just like you said."

Her heart resumed beating, slamming into her rib cage. "Well... That's good. That's all right, then."

"Yeah, that's great. Only I think you got the amount wrong."

"No," she said sharply. "That's what we agreed to."

"Sure. Only we reached that agreement, you know, before you sold the house. I was thinking now that Doug's estate is settled, you might be able to meet your obligations faster."

Rachel sucked in a deep breath, turning her back on her mother's uncomprehending stare, Sean's intent look. The receiver slipped in her sweaty palm. "No. I can't. I'm sorry, but I can't."

"Look, I've got obligations of my own, Mrs. Fuller. It's not good business for me to carry a debt on my books."

She swallowed. "Yes. And I appreciate your patience. But Doug had other commitments, too." Gambling losses. Hotel and casino bills. Unsecured loans. "I can't afford to give you more right now."

"Maybe you can't afford not to. You've got to consider there's more important things than money. There's family."

"Yes, I know what kind of 'family' you come from," Rachel snapped.

The voice chuckled. "That was cute, Mrs. Fuller. That was smart. You're a smart woman. Which is why I know you'll understand when I tell you it's your family you've got to be concerned about."

Terror coiled cold around her heart. She squeezed her eyes shut, as if she could block out his threat, force back her fear. "You leave my family out of this," she said fiercely.

A warm hand closed next to hers over the receiver.

Startled, she opened her eyes and found Sean MacNeill at her shoulder, broad and hard and close.

He plucked the phone from her. "I don't know who the hell you are," he growled. "And I don't give a damn what you want. You're annoying the lady. She's not taking your calls, and we've notified the police. Now bug off."

The receiver rattled into its cradle.

The police. Oh, my God. "How could you... What have you done?"

He raised an eyebrow. "I hung up. Don't fall over thanking me, now."

"I won't. Don't interfere. Please. You have no idea what you're getting involved in."

"Why don't you tell me?" he invited quietly.

She wanted to. She almost did. His eyes were steady and kind.

Was she out of her mind? Confiding in Sean could only result in danger for him and disappointment for her. And the threat of the police... Her heart pounded like a sprinter's. She had to protect her children. Bilotti had told her. Warned her. No police.

"You don't want to know," she said, moving away from the phone. Away from his solid chest and his warm persuasion.

"Try me."

Myra chimed in from the kitchen table, her eyes and tone anxious. "If something's wrong, you should let Sean help, Rachel."

Good old Mama. When in doubt, rely on the most unreliable male around.

"Everything's fine," Rachel insisted. "I can handle it."

From Myra's worried face and Sean's skeptical expression, it was clear they didn't believe her.

Rachel fought the lurch of fear. She didn't believe it herself.

Chapter 5

Sean frowned as the woman's voice—breathless, urgent, yearning—carried out to the porch.

"I need you," she said. "I'll always need you. Darling, please…"

"Does your antacid medicine work when you need it?" The announcer's rich voice rolled from the television inside.

Sean set another screw into the threshold of the front door. He'd never been a fan of daytime drama. But even before the commercial interruption, it was pretty clear that that guy on Myra's soap, that "Darling," was being taken for a chump.

Sean could sympathize.

He drilled the screw into the frame. Twelve years ago, Trina had told him she needed him, too. Only to decide, when his chance at graduation was gone and his college plans were shot and his heart was irrevocably given to a three-month-old baby, that it was someone else she needed after all.

He shook his head. Definite chump behavior.

At least with Rachel Fuller, he'd never have to worry about being asked to take on more responsibility than he wanted.

I can handle it, she'd insisted.

Meaning, *Butt out, MacNeill.*

Fine by him. He'd never had to work for a woman's company or approval. He wasn't about to spoil his record for a stubborn high school teacher with two troubled brats.

A stubborn, *bossy* high school teacher. He checked the level of the door one more time before sinking the screws. It was Rachel's fault he was working on this door. Well, not her fault exactly. He'd offered his labor in lieu of rent. But in Rachel's zeal to protect her mother, she'd presented him with a list of household repairs that would have intimidated Bob Villa.

He targeted another screw. The drill whined and chugged. So, she looked out for her mother. Given his own close family ties, he could admire that. He could even appreciate her devotion to her kids. But they weren't his kids, and he wasn't getting involved.

Too bad he couldn't shake the memory of Rachel's white face that night he'd hung up the phone. She'd needed him then. At least, she'd needed somebody.

He set the drill down on the porch. Since Trina, he'd tried to stay out of the game until he knew the score. It was his tough luck Rachel tempted him to play.

He was caulking under the step when Myra Jordan's serviceable old Buick rumbled up the drive. It must be three-thirty already. He stood to stretch. The car's rear door opened and Rachel's daughter tumbled out, pale-legged, red-cheeked and furious.

He ambled to the top of the steps as she slammed the car door practically in her brother's face and stormed up the walk.

"Nice day?" he inquired dryly as she charged the porch.

"It stunk," she announced. "The kids here are all losers."

She stalked past him.

"Careful of the step," he said.

She threw him a scornful look and then lifted her foot with exaggerated care over the newly installed threshold. He could hear her stomping up the stairs.

The driver's door swung open. His breath jammed in his lungs as Rachel got out of the car in sections: her long, lovely legs beneath a midcalf-length skirt, her glossy dark hair pushed back by sunglasses, her oversize purse and a plain canvas bag thick with teacher stuff.

She looked tired.

Beneath the familiar, almost reassuring, tug of sex, he felt sympathy stir. She looked like she could use a long, cold glass of something—he pegged her as a white-wine-on-ice kind of girl—and a long, hot soak in the tub and a long, slow back rub. Naked.

Don't go there, chump.

Chris trailed up the baking concrete walk, his head low and his brand-new book bag dragging.

"How's it going, sport?"

The boy lifted one shoulder. "Okay."

Uh-oh. "You like your teacher? The other kids?"

The boy's gaze slid sideways. "They're all right, I guess."

Meaning, Sean reckoned, that the third graders of Davis Elementary had closed ranks against the Yankee invader.

"Give it time," he advised quietly. "It'll get better."

Chris nodded, but he didn't look up.

Rachel appeared on the step below her son. "Go on in the house, honey. Grandma will get you a snack."

She watched him disappear through the doorway, her smile too determined and her eyes too anxious. Sean felt another pluck of sympathy. "Are you sure about that?" she asked.

"That it'll get better? Oh, yeah," he said. "I'm a marine brat. I know."

She sighed. "Well, that's something. Thanks."

The words were pulled out of him. "Tough day?"

"I think we all had a case of new school nerves this morning. But it was nice to be back in a classroom again."

"If you say so."

"You didn't like school?"

Her assumption irritated him. Maybe he'd never been a boy genius like Con, but there had been a time.... No regrets, Sean reminded himself.

"Not enough to finish."

Her teeth worried her full bottom lip. "I could help you," she offered suddenly. "If you wanted to study at home, I mean."

"Thanks. But—"

She spoke over him, her big eyes earnest, her voice urgent. General Rachel on campaign. It was cute. "You could still get your G.E.D. There are books—"

He'd earned his General Equivalency Diploma almost ten years ago. "No, thanks."

"It could help you find another job."

"No. Thanks. I don't want another job. Not right away, anyway."

Her brow furrowed. "Doesn't it bother you not to have a steady paycheck?"

"Some. But it bothered me more, working for some bozo who couldn't tell an awl from his— Well, anyway, I've been working construction for twelve years. I'm in no rush."

"So, you're just going to…hang around?"

"Maybe. Didn't you ever want to take some time off, Rachel?"

He could see her eyes widen with the possibilities. But she shook her head. "And do what?"

He shrugged. "Whatever you wanted. Sleep in late. Go on a picnic or to the movies. Take a break. Take a chance." He took a step closer, enjoying the hitch of her breath and the scent of her hair. "Make love in a hammock."

Rachel fought the longing he conjured with his words. She was the grown-up. She didn't have time for hammocks. "Parade around in silly T-shirts?" she asked dryly.

He glanced down at his chest. "You've got a problem with my T-shirt?"

"'Smile, It's The Second Best Thing You Can Do With Your Lips'?" She rolled her eyes. "Oh, please. You don't think that's a little suggestive? There are children around. My children."

"It was a gift."

"You're not blaming your sister-in-law again."

"Absolutely. I wouldn't have put smiling that high on the list, myself. Third, maybe."

She looked at that clever, mobile mouth and wondered just what those lips could do to earn the top two spots on his list. Oh, dear Heaven. Her heart bumped.

She forced her gaze up from his warmly smiling mouth and found his eyes bright with amusement.

"Talking," he said. "That would have to be number

two. The Irish are all big talkers. And aren't you the silly one now?''

"You set me up."

"Maybe. But from where I stand it's not the children we need to worry about getting the wrong idea."

"Don't flatter yourself, MacNeill."

"Yes, Teacher."

"And don't make fun of me."

"Hey." He stooped to peer at her face, frowned. "That wasn't making fun. That was banter."

His sudden concern brought an absurd ache to the back of her throat. She ducked her head. "Sorry. My bantering skills are a little rusty."

"That's okay. You can practice on me anytime."

Temptation dried her mouth. She moistened her lips. "So generous. And you have all that experience."

"My share."

"More than your share, I'd guess. Do you ever get your women mixed up?"

His eyes narrowed, but he responded easily. "Maybe I would, if I thought of them as 'my women' instead of as individuals I like to spend time with."

His sincerity abashed her. "I'm sorry." She sighed. "I seem to be doing a lot of apologizing today."

"Now, see, that's not on the list at all."

"Excuse me?"

"Apologizing," he explained. "It's not on the lips list. Let's see if we can't come up with something better."

Confusion backed up her breathing. It was just more banter, she told herself, watching his head descend. She was getting the wrong idea again, because he was sexy—beautiful, really, in a wholly masculine way, with his sin-dark eyes and perfect nose and luxurious hair—and close. Temptingly close. She kept her eyes open. That hard, handsome face blurred. It was almost as if he really intended to...

Kiss her.

Sean took his time, gliding his hands over and around her, feeling the smooth column of her waist and the moist heat of her skin under the proper blouse she wore. Nice. He aligned their bodies slowly, giving her time to draw back or participate, whatever she wanted.

She was tall. Even standing on the step below him, her head was on the level with his chin. He liked that, he decided, liked the way her curves fit his angles as he pulled her closer.

Not too close, he cautioned himself. Not too tight. Nothing too sudden, to scare her away. Her eyes were wide enough already. He could see the clear whites of them and flecks of green deep in the brown.

He closed his own and slid into the kiss. Her lips were moist and closed. She smelled damn good for a schoolteacher, like the warm scents in the air after she showered. The thought aroused him. The taste of her aroused him, and the warmth of her full breasts touching his chest, and the solid feel of her rib cage under his hands.

When she didn't protest, when she didn't pull away, he added pressure, teasing her lips apart. Her stubborn mouth was full and soft. Her tart tongue was sweet and velvet.

Oh, *yeah,* he thought. And then her breath shuddered into his mouth, and her hands tightened in his hair, and he didn't think at all.

He'd only intended to provoke her, to soothe her, to kiss her as he'd kissed a hundred or more women before. He wasn't prepared for the leap of hunger or the surge of possession. The two together battered at his practiced smoothness, tore from him an unexpected and not entirely welcome response.

Hot. Rachel Fuller was hot. And Sean was getting hotter by the second.

He changed angles and went deep, losing himself in her, like an explorer in the jungle tempted off familiar paths by the exotic. He was lured by the lush textures of her, dazed by the sudden rise in temperature. His heart pounded. His blood drummed in his head. And she cooperated, damn it, sucked him in, pulled him to her with those smooth, strong arms and devoured him as much as he was devouring her.

The drumbeat in his ears escalated and ran together in one long blare.

He ignored it. Ignored that they were standing in full view on her mother's front porch with her children inside the house. Ignored that he was grimy with sweat and sawdust and marking her pretty blouse. Ignored that desire was supposed to be a pastime and a pleasure and not a need fisting his gut...

Rachel's hands slid from his hair to his shoulders and pushed, too hard to be ignored.

Reluctantly he raised his head, separating from her in degrees: tongue, lips, torso. She looked almost as dazed as he felt, he noted with a spurt of masculine satisfaction. Her pupils were wide. Her mouth looked wet and well-kissed.

But she was already going away from him, rearranging her face in her schoolteacher's mask. She ran her tongue over already slick lips, glanced over her shoulder and back.

"You have company," she said.

"What?"

"One of the individuals you like to spend time with

just pulled into the driveway.'' Her voice was careful, dry. Was she mocking him or herself?

He looked, and there was Lori Tucker, leaning on the steering wheel of her red Miata, pulled up to the concrete walk behind Myra Jordan's old Buick.

The blare. A car horn. Right.

Aw, hell.

It should have been funny. Maybe with another woman it would have been funny. Growing up, there had always been enough women hanging around the old frame house in Quincy to keep all the MacNeill brothers busy. This certainly wasn't the first time two of Sean's had bumped into one another coming or going. He usually handled such encounters with a rueful grace that kept his partners civil, if not satisfied.

But right now, with his body at the ready and his mind blown and Rachel's eyes flat with hurt, Sean wasn't up to handling anything.

She handled it for him, and that was maybe worse.

Stepping away from him, she tugged at the waist of her white blouse, restoring order. Composure. Distance.

''Hello,'' she said. ''You must be here to see Sean. He's all yours.''

She opened the screen door and went in, her straight back disappearing into the shadows of the house.

Lori sauntered down the walk, moving well on her three-inch heels. Sean appreciated the picture she made, even as it failed to grab him at the level Rachel did in her long skirt and sensible school shoes.

Stopping at the bottom of the steps, Lori waved a white envelope at him. ''I brought you your last paycheck.''

He reached and stuffed it into his back jeans' pocket. ''Thanks. I take it Walt wants me off the site, huh?''

''You got it, big guy.'' She raised penciled eyebrows.

"So, I guess you're not going to be coming around anymore."

She was talking about more than the job, and they both knew it. Sean was grateful for the tactful exit. But then, they'd both known going in that there would be good times and no strings.

"Looks like it," he said.

"Well." She hesitated, shading her eyes with one hand against the sun. "It's been fun."

"Yeah, it has." As she turned on her stiletto heels to go, he took one long stride off the porch and stopped her with a hand on her arm. "Lori...thanks."

"Anytime, big guy. Call me, if you get free." She waggled her fingers at him. "Bye."

Was he out of his mind? Why was he exchanging a neat little package like Lori for the messy bundle of warmth and responsibilities that was Rachel?

Assuming he was making any such exchange. He didn't know what significance their full-body-contact kiss carried for Rachel.

Heck, he didn't know what to make of it himself. His body yelled, *Full speed ahead,* and his mind screamed, *Turn back now.* But whether he listened to his body or his mind, it wasn't fair to Lori to pretend his attention was with her right now.

So he watched the real estate agent twitch down the walk in her pretty power suit and wondered what the hell he was doing.

One kiss didn't mean anything, Rachel lectured herself as she wrung out the children's wet washcloths and folded them over the towel bar by the sink. Sean probably kissed women all the time. He probably did more than that with the tousled-haired shark who'd strutted up her sidewalk.

It was Rachel's own fault that she was so lonely, so desperately in need of comfort, that she imagined Sean's kiss was something more than a knee-jerk response to any breathing female wearing mascara.

She caught a glimpse of herself in the mirror above the sink and winced. Her own mascara, carefully applied for school, had smudged, leaving big bags under her eyes. She looked tired and felt about a hundred years old.

I'm ancient, she'd told him the first night they'd met, and it was true.

She was tired. She was sick of being scared and weary of managing by herself. But that was no excuse for fantasizing about her mother's boarder. A twenty-nine-year-old, out-of-work carpenter with an earring couldn't help her, no matter how broad his shoulders were. Maybe mailing her monthly check to Carmine Bilotti had been enough to satisfy the racketeer. Maybe Sean's blunt intervention hadn't provoked him into sending the debt collectors after her like Hollywood hit men. Maybe. And maybe she was as blind as an owl in daytime because she didn't want to see what a mistake it would be to get involved with somebody like Sean MacNeill.

What did she tell her high school students? Sex doesn't solve your problems. It just hands you a whole set of new ones.

She pulled a face at the mirror. Let them put *that* on a T-shirt.

Rinsing the toothpaste from the sink, she went along the hall to kiss her children good-night.

Chris bounced into bed as she came through the door. Rachel smiled. "Teeth all brushed?"

"Yep."

She glanced at the narrow empty bed on the other side of the room. "Where's Lindsey?"

"I, uh..."

Secrets, again. They were everywhere, wrapped around the fragile pieces of their lives like the paper they'd used to pack up the contents of the old house. *Don't tell on Lindsey. Don't worry the children. Don't burden Mama.*

"Chris," she warned.

He squirmed under the covers. "She went to see Sean."

Oh, no. "To see Mr. MacNeill? Why?"

"Well, you said I shouldn't bother him anymore. And I finished that comic book, and I thought maybe he'd let me have another one."

And so he'd begged or bribed Xena Warrior Pre-Teen into marching over there for him. Rachel sighed. "Oh, Chris."

"You didn't say she couldn't."

"No, but I thought you both understood... Never mind." Why should her children be any more able to resist Sean than she was?

She brushed Chris's hair back from his face and kissed his forehead. "'Night, honey. God bless you."

"God bless." His arms came around her neck.

Tears rushed to her eyes at the simple contact. Oh, God, she was some kind of emotional mess when a reminder of past cuddles could make her weepy. No wonder she'd been all over Sean MacNeill. She was obviously starved for human contact.

How humiliating.

"Sleep tight," she said with effort, and went to collect her daughter.

Myra was singing softly along with the radio in the kitchen. Rachel opened the screen door—it didn't stick anymore—and stepped over the newly installed threshold onto the porch. She could almost hear her mother say it. *So nice to have a man around the house.*

And it was, damn it. Nice to have the gutters cleaned and the dripping faucet silenced and the radiator level checked on her mother's car. Nice to meet his wicked dark eyes in the morning and hide her blush behind a coffee cup, and feel, for brief seconds, as if she wasn't one of the walking dead.

She stood a moment, letting her eyes adjust to the moonless night. Above the dark trees a nimbus of humidity wrapped each star, and from them, a chorus of cicadas rose and fell like the sea at high tide. The big overhead doors of the garage stood open, spilling light and paint fumes and admitting the warm evening breeze.

Bugs, too, probably, Rachel thought, deliberately resisting the pull of the soft summer night.

But mosquitoes didn't seem to bother the man kneeling on the tarp-covered floor. Under the white shop lights, Sean was painting a tall, narrow cupboard with even brush strokes, his face hard with concentration and his dark hair escaping its stubby ponytail.

Yearning took her by the throat, not so much for the man as for the girl who might have let herself fall for him, the girl who might have believed in that teasing smile and those concerned eyes and the strength implicit in his wrists and his voice.

Stupid, Rachel scolded herself. She hadn't been that girl for a long time now. She started down the walk.

She was halfway to the gravel drive when she spotted Lindsey, like a ghost from her own childhood, curled up on the dragon-claw sofa, watching Sean paint.

"You're dripping," Lindsey said.

The brush lifted, paused, and then resumed. "No, I'm not. Don't you have homework to do?"

"You asked me that already. I finished."

"Didn't take you long."

"No. It was easy. The kids here are really dumb."

Rachel bit her lip in distress. It had been a tough week for all of them, but toughest for Lindsey. "Fifth graders rule!" she'd crowed last June, with summer spread before her and a return to her old school at the end of it. She wasn't in command at Davis Elementary; and Rachel knew her daughter felt the loss of power keenly.

Sean continued to stroke paint on the cupboard, his attention apparently on his work. "Dumb, how?"

"Just dumb." When that failed to get a response, Lindsey elaborated. "They're all a bunch of hicks, anyway. Brittany Lewis made fun of my notebook. And Heather Mills said I talk funny."

"You do." When she glared at him, Sean shrugged. "So do I. All us Yankees sound different to them."

"Not Mom." Lindsey's voice was accusing. "Since we got here she sounds just like Grandma."

"Not exactly," Sean said, but Lindsey wasn't listening.

"I hate it here," she said. "There's nobody I like and nothing to do."

Rachel's heart constricted.

Sean's brush moved up and down. "There's a Labor Day carnival in town on Saturday," he said at last.

Lindsey rolled her eyes. "Oh, whoopee."

She waited. He didn't reply.

"Would you take me?" she asked in a small voice.

Sean dipped his brush in the paint can. "Hell, no. Maybe you should try being nice to your mom for a change, see if she will."

"But I won't know anybody."

"So, it takes time to make new friends."

"I don't want new friends."

"Well, with an attitude like that you won't have to worry about it, will you?"

Rachel, listening in the darkness, stiffened in her child's defense.

But Lindsey grinned. "You stink," she said amiably.

Sean raised his eyebrows. "That's the paint, dollface."

Their momentary rapport made Rachel uncomfortable. Lindsey still wasn't over the loss of her father. She couldn't afford to fall for a transient carpenter with a commitment problem.

And neither could Rachel.

She stepped forward into the swathe of light, trying for casual even when the words stuck in her throat like crackers. "Here you are, sweetie. I thought I told you the garage was off-limits for now."

Lindsey squirmed. "You told *Chris*."

"Which naturally brought her out here hot-foot to see what the big attraction was," Sean said.

But Rachel already knew what—or rather, who—the attraction was. Averting her gaze from his hard, broad shoulders, she said politely, "I hope she didn't interrupt your work."

He waved his paintbrush at her. "Not too much."

"Well…" She stood uncertainly. "Thank you. Lindsey, bedtime."

Her daughter's lower lip protruded. "I don't have to go to bed yet."

"It's almost nine-twenty."

"I don't want to go to bed."

"Show's over, kid," Sean said. "Scoot. Take the comic book with you."

Lindsey tossed her head and scrambled off the couch. With a look at her mother—*I'm going, but you didn't make me*—she scooted.

Sean set his brush across the can of red paint. He stood slowly, wiping his hands on his thighs. Rachel's mouth went dry. The gesture called attention to, oh, to everything: his height and his lazy grace and the way his damn jeans fit. God save her from a man with a high, tight butt in a pair of well-washed denims.

She looked up to meet his wicked dark gaze, and her cheeks burned.

''You wanted me?'' he drawled.

Chapter 6

He stood there with the shop lights throwing his body into bold relief, sliding over the muscles revealed by his sleeveless T-shirt.

Rachel couldn't do anything about the color burning her cheeks, but she'd be damned before she'd gulp. She cleared her throat instead. "Nice line. Does it work often?"

Humor flashed in his eyes. It was hard not to like a man who could laugh at himself.

"You'd be surprised," he said.

"Not really," she muttered.

"What?"

"I really came to get Lindsey. I hope the children aren't bothering you."

"Not much." He took a step closer. "Not like you do."

The safest way—the only way—to deal with that was to ignore it. She retreated, skirting the edges of the tarp-covered floor to his workbench. His tools hung in orderly rows, arranged by size. His organized work space contrasted with his dangerous looks, his half-bare chest and raffish earring. Who was he? The conscientious workman or the careless pirate? Her heart tripped faster. Which did she want him to be?

"I was thinking about what you said. About Chris needing a chance to get away from the house?"

"From the henhouse, I said."

It was payback, she decided, for her "nice line" crack. She waved it off. "Anyway, I never meant he couldn't even see you to return a comic book. If you don't mind him stopping by…"

"I told you I don't mind."

She turned to face him. "No power tools, though."

He took another step nearer. "No. Rachel…"

Her back was up against the workbench. She grasped the edge with both hands, determined to keep control of the subject and herself. Chris. They were talking about her son.

"Both children saw a therapist after Doug—after. Chris seemed to be coping."

He dipped his head. A strand of his hair slipped close to her cheek. His breath tickled her ear. "Coping is good."

Her eyelids felt weighted. She fought to keep them open, like a child struggling against sleep. Like a swimmer in danger of drowning. "Yes. But he's been very… It seems silly to complain, but he's been almost too quiet. Too obedient. That's why I was so surprised when he did that awful thing to your chair."

"He's dealing with a move and a whole new set of rules and people. He's probably just…" His warm lips brushed her cheekbone. "…acting up for attention."

She inhaled sharply, smelling paint and lumber and man. "That doesn't mean you should put yourself out."

"I won't."

"We can manage on our own."

"Sure." His mouth glided down to the curve of her jaw, found the pulse point just below her ear. "But if there's anything I can do to help…"

It wasn't just the suggestion of sex in his voice that loosened her knees and made her go all soft and liquid inside. It was the undernote of humor, the promise of shared fun. As if, as long as he held her, she could shed the worried caretaker with tired eyes who'd taken control of her mirror and become someone else. Someone a gorgeous man in a sleeveless T-shirt could tease and make love with. Someone warm and urgent and alive she might have been once upon a time.

Someone stupid.

This time she did gulp. "I think you've probably done enough."

"Lady, I am just getting started."

She knew better than to let him. Really, she did. But when he rested one hand alongside hers on the workbench, her arm prickled at the nearness of his. Her body shivered at his closeness. Little zings and tingles chased under her skin, calling attention to places she'd neglected for months. Years. He pulled back and met her gaze, with laughter and something else in his eyes, and she noticed that his lashes were unfairly long and thick for a man's and that he needed a shave. Common sense screamed at her to be good, to be careful, to get back inside the house where she belonged.

Rachel stayed right where she was.

He leaned into her and kissed the arch of her brow and the space between her eyebrows where her headache lurked and the tip of her nose. His breath was warm and coffee-scented. His lips were soft and practiced. Every place his mouth touched set up a little chorus of agreement that drowned out the cautionary voices in her head. Yes. You betcha. Please.

She waited for him to get on with it. She wasn't making this difficult. He probably didn't have much time to spend seducing a thirty-four-year-old widow and mother of two. But he continued to caress her face with slow, warm, open kisses, slowly leaching the tension from her muscles and building the anticipation under her skin. Her heart tripped faster. She was either going to jump him or lose her nerve.

She turned her head abruptly, engaging that tempting mouth. With a jolt, he complied with her silent demand, giving her his heat, filling her with the slick pressure of his tongue, bringing her up close against his long, warm body. He felt solid and strong against her. He felt aroused, and she closed her eyes at the wicked pleasure of it, the pleasure of arousing him.

They kissed, progressively slower. Deeper. Wetter. He tasted so good she could actually tune out the busy whispers in her head, blanket them with the electric sensations of body-to-body contact. He was reassuringly hard. She felt her insides contracting and her breasts tightening in need. It was almost like an itch, insistent, impossible to ignore. She rubbed against him, and he groaned encouragement into her mouth.

His hands moved over her, his wide-palmed, long-fingered hands. He closed one over her breast as if he knew what she needed. She almost whimpered in relief as his blunt, clever fingers stroked and shaped and tugged.

With his hand between their bodies, their hips pressed closer together. She tried to widen her legs, but the workbench was hard against her back and he was tight against her front. She made a small, frustrated sound in her throat and wiggled in protest.

His free hand fisted in her hair and pulled their fused mouths apart.

His eyes were dark and hot. "What do you want to do?"

"I..."

"What do you want, Rachel?"

As if he actually saw her. As if what she wanted mattered.

And she knew, with enormous regret, that the Rachel reflected in his eyes absolutely could not go through with...with whatever she'd thought she was about to do.

The change must have registered in her face, because his mouth tightened. His grip in her hair loosened.

"Lose your nerve?" he asked, almost sympathetically.

It was so close to what she'd actually been thinking that her denial died unspoken. "That, or my mind."

"Want me to try to change it for you?"

She was almost unbearably tempted to say yes, to let him take over, to let him take the responsibility for what happened between them. She shook her head. "I need to go in."

"Running away?"

"Certainly not," she lied. "Lindsey will be waiting for me to tuck her in."

"I could wait for you to tuck me in, too. If you want to come back."

"It's not a question of what I want. I have obligations."

"Responsible Rachel." Was he making fun of her? But his eyes were warm.

"Yes," she said baldly.

His knuckle brushed her cheek. "Okay. Good night."

She swallowed disappointment. "You're taking this awfully well."

He laughed shortly. "Beautiful, I'm hard enough right now to pound nails. But nothing's going to happen you're not ready for."

His blunt admission was as arousing as his touch, his consideration more devastating than his kisses. Both made it even harder to walk away. But she did.

She walked back alone, feeling his gaze like a hand on the small of her back. She didn't turn around. When she reached the porch she could hear the rumble of a police drama from her mother's TV and Lindsey shouting at the top of the stairs for Chris to get out of the bathroom.

This was what she had. This was all she had. It was time she made the best of it.

Taking a sharp breath, Rachel pulled on the screen door and went inside the house.

The town of Benson's Labor Day celebration wasn't a bad fair, Sean thought, strolling the makeshift midway. Not as neighborly as the parish carnival at St. Ann's, not as big as the old Marshfield Fair south of Boston, but it had all the required elements: a rickety row of game booths, a 4-H exhibit, and a lot full of rattletrap rides. In the field below the high school, a rash of craft tents had sprung up like mushrooms after a rain.

A fire truck gleamed to a spit-polish shine and bicycles decorated with crepe paper were parked on the sidewalk in front of the school. The marching band had already performed on the main stage. A row of little girls in sparkling leotards twirled for their parents on the platform, and a sandwich board announced the Starlight Swing Band scheduled for seven o'clock.

Yeah, a good fair. And since breaking up with Lori

Tucker, it was the closest thing to excitement Sean was likely to find. Despite his outsider status in town, he was enjoying the racing kids and the waving flags, the smell of grilling sausages, the pastel puffs of cotton candy and the bright lights of the Ferris wheel doing their valiant best against the sunshine and dingy paint.

Of course, normally he'd have somebody beside him to share it all with, to squeal on the roller coaster and give him a reason to try for one of the giant prizes hanging from the booths. Somebody female, and older than his niece Brianna. But Lori was history, and the only other candidate had made it plain she wasn't in his future.

He stopped at one of the stands to buy beer in a plastic cup. He'd had a close escape there, he thought. Rachel, with her warm eyes and her hot mouth and her stubborn independent streak, had blown his cool and his mind. Even the memory of her, eager and strong in his arms, made him ache. A woman like that could make him forget every rule he had about dating women with kids. Yeah, a real close escape, he told himself, and tried to ignore the nagging emptiness he felt.

In the meantime, drinking a cold beer in the hot sun with dust and straw and popcorn underfoot was a thousand times better than sitting alone in a bar.

And he didn't have to stay alone. With more experience than purpose, he eyed the holiday crowd. Pretty teens in skinny tank tops. Too young. A chattering group in lawn chairs, their flowered skirts bright in the shade. Too old. A good-humored, sharp-featured policewoman patrolling the fair gave him a nod and got a smile in return. There was a nice-looking blonde at the bake sale stall and a glossy brunette with great legs leaning over the counter at the milk can toss....

Rachel.

Before he could think better of it, he crossed the midway to her side.

Chris had won a plush green dog, and Lindsey was wild with wanting one.

"Please, Mommy. Pleeeease? Just one more. Let me try just one more time."

Mommy. Not Mom. Rachel smiled down into her daughter's pink-cheeked, pleading face. It was worth the money already gone on games and greasy food, worth the hours she would be up preparing lesson plans tomorrow night. Definitely worth another fifty cents for a chance to knock the milk cans down.

"Well..." she drawled, pretending to consider.

The booth attendant, an old hand at spotting an easy mark, plunked three balls down on the counter. "Here ya go."

"Yes!" Lindsey crowed, and made a grab for them.

Rachel dug in her shorts' pocket for her shrinking wad of tickets. "Take your time. Aim."

Lindsey nodded, weighing the ball in her hand, judging the distance to her target. She threw. The top four cans tumbled.

"Good girl!" Rachel said. Chris jumped up and down.

Lindsey glowed. She threw again. Another can fell, leaving five: a straight row across the bottom and one on top.

"I can't do it," Lindsey said.

But she tried. Her ball sailed uselessly to the right of the top can and smacked into the canvas at the back of the booth. Her shoulders slumped.

"Not bad," a male voice said appraisingly behind them. "A little lower and you would have taken them down."

Rachel recognized that lazy, deep voice. Her heart thud-ded. She turned and saw Sean, thumbs stuck in his jeans' front pockets, dark hair brushing the back of his neck, earring winking like a promise. He grinned as if he were glad just to see her, and she grinned foolishly, helplessly, back.

"Sean!" Chris said.

He nodded. "Hey, sport."

"Can you hit them?" Lindsey demanded. "I want a dog."

Rachel pulled herself together. "Lindsey, it's not polite to ask—"

"'S okay. It's a male prerogative, winning prizes for pretty girls at fairs."

"Don't be sexist. I could get one for her."

He tipped his head back, regarding her from under thick, dark lashes. "Could you now? Care to make a bet?"

Ridiculously, her heart beat faster. Was this how Doug felt, she wondered, when the stakes were raised? "What kind of bet?"

"A friendly one. I win the prize, you let me take you and the kids around."

It sounded like fun, she thought wistfully. She raised her eyebrows, proud of her control. "I thought you limited yourself to women without responsibilities?"

He'd said that to her, Sean remembered. He'd meant it, too. He shrugged. "So, change the bet. I win, you give me a dance when the band comes on tonight."

"And if I win?"

"You want to make this a competition? Fine. You win, I'll buy you all a bunch of tickets."

She looked uncertain. "I don't gamble."

"It's not gambling. It's a sure thing. Either way, the kid gets the dog."

"Do it, Mom," Lindsey urged.

"Yeah, do it," said Chris.

Rachel caught her lower lip in her teeth, plainly torn. Excited. Sean's body tightened. He wouldn't have minded getting a good bite of that mouth himself.

"You've got yourself a bet," she said, and slapped down two tickets.

He grinned. "You take cash?" he asked the guy behind the counter.

The attendant shifted his toothpick to the other side of his mouth, considering. "I'll hold your money. You turn it in for tickets when you're done."

"Great. Thanks."

There were two pyramids of wooden "milk cans" behind the plank counter, ten to a stack.

Rachel picked up a ball and looked at Sean.

He gestured. "Ladies first."

She nodded once, all business-like. Affectionate laughter rose silently in his throat. She looked so cute, with her earnest face and her dark hair escaping from its ponytail. She took a step back. He just had time to admire her hips in her neat cuffed shorts before she let a missile fly. Seven cans scattered, and the laughter sank into astonishment.

She turned to him, satisfaction gleaming in her eyes. "Your turn."

Piece of cake. He hefted the ball in his hand, measured the distance to the target with his eyes, and threw. The ball hit slightly off center with enough power behind it to take down most of the piled cans. He counted. Seven.

Rachel's lips moved as she counted, too. She picked up her next ball. He watched her long fingers curl around it, and the sleek strength of her arm as she coiled and launched the ball. He shook his head. She was arousing him without even trying. Without even looking at him.

He heard the kids whoop and checked out her target. All three cans were down.

He raised an eyebrow. "Nice throw."

"Do I win?"

"He— Heck, no. I still have two shots."

It took both, and he was really trying. When the last can went flying, he turned to her in triumph. She was laughing.

The booth attendant set two tiny plush toys on the counter. "That wins you each a small prize. Want to go again?"

Sean bared his teeth in a grin. "Two out of three?"

She tossed her head. "You're on."

"Go, Mom," said Lindsey.

Her first shot toppled eight cans and left two teetering.

"You," Sean told her solemnly, "are a dangerous woman."

She beamed at him, cheeks flushed, the tip of her tongue escaping from between her lips, delighted as a child on Christmas morning. Something huge and soft expanded in his chest, forcing his breath out in a whoosh. *Dangerous.* Yes. In ways he was only beginning to discover.

Their competition was attracting a small hometown crowd. From two rows back, a kid called, "Way to go, Mrs. Fuller!" and her face flushed an even prettier pink.

Sean turned to look at the boy, a blond, muscled teen in a flannel shirt worn open over his white T-shirt. Cocky. Hot.

"One of your students?" he guessed.

"Nick Cooper. How did you know?"

"I recognize the type. Hell, I used to *be* the type."

He was delighted when she laughed again; less delighted when she nailed her remaining cans with one ball and he needed two.

"Bad luck," Rachel said sympathetically.

He was either going to kiss her or strangle her. "Thanks. Again."

She looked almost guilty. "Oh, I don't think—"

"Come on, Mrs. Fuller!" a girl shouted.

"I want a big dog, Mommy."

"You go first this time," she said.

To make him feel better, he thought, in case he needed the extra turn again. Her scruples tickled him.

"Lose your nerve?" he teased, deliberately echoing his earlier challenge.

Her chin went up. "Maybe I just want to study your form."

Yep, he was definitely going to have to kiss her. Or hit something. He eyed the stacked milk cans. Redirected energy, his old shop teacher called it. He fired the ball. Milk cans exploded in every direction. All ten of them.

"Very nice," Rachel approved. "Did you play baseball?"

He grinned. "Little League. You?"

"Fast-pitch softball. Four years in high school."

And she turned and drilled the ball at her target. Two shots, and she'd cleared the stack.

The attendant spat out his toothpick. "She's a match for you, buddy."

"Yeah," Sean said slowly. "You could be right."

"Two!" Lindsey shrieked as the man reached for the pole that hooked down the big prizes.

"Chris gets one," Rachel said immediately.

"But who won?" the boy wanted to know.

"I don't know." Her dark eyes sought Sean's, oddly uncertain. "It's a draw, I guess. Nobody won."

"We both won," Sean contradicted her. "Let me get your tickets."

"You don't have to. You can't afford—"

He held up a hand to stop her. He wasn't any more strapped for cash than she was. "I can treat the kids to a couple of spins on the Ferris wheel. Besides—" He winked. "I can't have you thinking I welsh on my bets."

Now what had he said to make her look so stricken?

"Be right back," he promised, and strode off to buy the tickets before she thought up some other objection.

When he got back, Chris was clutching a giant red bull dog while his sister stroked a three-foot-tall dalmatian in a fireman's hat. At Sean's approach, the girl looked up and smiled almost shyly. He felt a twinge of an old pain like a splinter working its way to his heart.

"Do you like him?" she asked.

If Trina had stayed with him, their daughter—her daughter—would be a year older than Lindsey now. Sean set his jaw. He wasn't going to get mixed up with these kids, no matter how attracted he was to their mother.

"Yeah. Cute." He thrust the roll of tickets at Rachel. "Seven o'clock."

"Excuse me?"

"The band starts playing at seven. I'll meet you at the main stage."

"I can't leave the children."

"So, bring them."

"I don't know…"

"One dance, Rachel," he said stubbornly, afraid he might start begging. Terrified she would refuse. "You owe me."

She winced. "Don't say that."

"Why not?"

Chris bumped his mother's arm. "Mom, can we ride on the roller coaster now?"

"Here." Sean tugged a strip of tickets from Rachel's hand and gave them to Lindsey. "See that dart toss? Right there? Want to take your brother over there for a minute while I talk with your mom?"

"Yeah!" Chris shouted.

"Sure."

"Stay where I can see you," Rachel called after them.

Sean turned back to her, trapping her against the side of the booth. "Don't say what? What's the problem?"

"I don't want to owe you." She ducked her head, so that her hair brushed his chin. He liked that she was tall, liked that he could indulge himself so easily in the scent of her, women's shampoo and essence of Rachel. She looked up, her dark eyes devastating at short range. "I've spent the past year worrying what I owe other people and I—well, I'm sick of it."

He didn't think she was talking just about money. "Okay. So, it's not what you owe me. How about what you owe yourself?"

Her breath was ragged. "I'm fine."

"Are you?" He crowded her a little, letting her feel his heat. "You've got a lot of people looking to you. Your mother. Your kids. It's admirable. I admire you like hell, all right? But don't you ever need a break?"

"Maybe it's not easy for someone like you to understand, but I take my responsibilities seriously."

"'Someone like me'?" he repeated softly. "What does that mean?"

"Well, someone single."

"Or childless? Unemployed, maybe?"

Her gaze dropped. Damn. That was it, then. Funny how

her opinion hurt. He was suddenly tired of being stamped like low-grade lumber. But he wasn't about to start offering explanations or excuses for the way he lived his life.

He straightened from the flimsy plywood wall. ''Guess I'll take my irresponsible ass out of your way then. But if you decide you want something different, beautiful—a break, a shoulder, a good time—I'll be waiting on the main stage at seven.''

Chapter 7

Rachel glanced across the picnic table at her children, at Lindsey, her arm stretched around the plush dalmatian, and Chris, using the last of his French fries to shovel catsup. They were having fun. She was glad. She owed it to them for having a daddy who went and killed himself and a mama who dragged them a million miles from anyplace they wanted to be and then had panic attacks every time the phone rang. She owed them.

How about what you owe yourself?

Rachel took a hasty swallow of watered-down Coke and choked.

Chris paused with a fry halfway to his mouth. Lindsey patted her arm. "You okay, Mom?"

Her heart swelled with love. "Fine."

And she would be, too. She'd pay off Bilotti and save up enough for them to move into their own apartment. Her children would have safety, security, stability.

The last thing her babies needed was for their mother

to form a temporary attachment to an inappropriate man. Rachel frowned at the melting ice in her cup. Or was it an inappropriate attachment to a temporary man? Either way, they didn't need it. She didn't need him.

"Rachel? Is that you?"

She jumped like a jock caught dozing in class and then smiled. Because that voice belonged to Deedee Pittman the algebra teacher, as close to a friend as Rachel had made since moving home. She swiveled on the splintery seat and watched as Deedee crossed the picnic ground, reminding Rachel of a robin with her black eyes and bright blouse, big chest and chirpy good humor.

"It's good to see you here. I thought you were going to tell me on Monday you got all tangled up in lesson plans." Deedee cocked her head to one side. "These your kids?"

Rachel smiled with pride. "Yes. Lindsey and Chris, this is Mrs. Pittman, who teaches with me at the high school."

They eyed her, Lindsey warily and Chris with disinterest. "Hi," they mumbled.

"I've got a girl about your age," Deedee said. "Jaclyn. You the new girl in her class she's been talking about?"

Lindsey brightened. "Jackie? Is she here?"

"She's about to get on the Ferris wheel with her daddy. You want to ride with them?"

"Can I go?" Chris asked.

"No," Lindsey said.

"I don't see why not," Deedee said at the same time, "seeing as how Jaclyn's got her little brothers with her. They're right down there, by the ticket stand, see?"

Chris hopped up from the picnic bench. "I see them!"

"Now, wait a minute," Rachel said, feeling her family slipping away. "We don't want to impose…"

"Mo-om," Lindsey groaned.

"Let 'em go," Deedee advised. "Rick's got his hands full, anyway. He won't notice two more. He'll take the boys, and the girls can go on their own."

"Is it—" Rachel broke off, uncertain how to ask her question without giving offense.

"—safe?" Deedee finished for her. "Honey, this is Benson. The kids'll be fine. Do them some good, if you ask me."

She was right. Wasn't that one of the reasons Rachel had come home, so that her children could do ordinary things without their mother acting weird and terror-stricken?

"I guess it would be all right," she said. "But I want you two back in twenty minutes, okay?"

Deedee shifted comfortably. "Give 'em an hour. You don't know what the lines are like. And maybe they'll want an ice cream or something."

"An hour, then," Rachel conceded.

"Ice cream!" Chris whooped.

Released, her children flew down the hill toward the prospect of friends and fun and the Ferris wheel. They looked like any of the other kids racing over the grass. They looked happy.

"Well." Rachel forced a laugh from her suddenly aching throat. "I feel unnecessary."

"About time." Deedee smiled to take the force from her words. "I've got to get going myself. I promised I'd put in an hour at the bake sale booth."

"Can I give you a hand?"

"Bless your heart, no. You're a single woman. You go carry on and enjoy yourself."

"This is Benson." Rachel repeated her friend's reminder dryly. "Not many opportunities for carrying on here."

"Band's starting," Deedee offered. "You could find yourself a nice 4-H boy and dance."

Rachel laughed. And then Sean's words slid into her mind, tempting as the serpent in Eden. *If you decide you want something different—a break, a shoulder, a good time—I'll be waiting on the main stage at seven.*

Twelve minutes later she found herself standing on the band platform with a racing heart and cold feet.

She was late.

She shouldn't have come at all.

The band was playing something she recognized as background music from her mother's radio. Only a handful of couples braved the platform's duct-taped seams and dangling Christmas lights. Yet the soft air fading into night and autumn wrapped music and lights in a hazy glow, transforming the makeshift dance floor into an outdoor ballroom.

Look at that young couple, showing off for each other the steps they must have learned for their wedding day. Or that pair of old pros, dancing with a grace and intimacy developed over years together. Tears pricked her eyes. She'd wanted that once, the closeness and the lifetime together. But Doug's gambling, and then his suicide, had killed her chance.

Did she really want to risk her dreams again?

A young man loomed in front of her, blocking her view of the dance floor. "Hiya, Mrs. Fuller."

She blinked hastily, but she still didn't recognize him. Above his well-developed arms and chest, his round head appeared to balance directly on his shoulders like a jack-o'-lantern on a brick wall. He wore dark slacks and a silk shirt open at the collar and a diamond earring. Not from around here, she thought.

"Do I know you?"

He offered her his broad, square hand. "Frank Bilotti. I work for my uncle Carmine."

Frank. The nephew. The one who got "carried away" when he'd robbed and then trashed her living room.

Her lips, her toes, her heart went numb. "What are you doing here?"

He squeezed her fingers. "I came to see you. My uncle, he's getting a little concerned about his investment."

"Gambling debt, you mean." She pulled her hand away. She resented his intrusion. It rankled that someone only half a dozen years older than her students could make her feel afraid. But she was terrified.

"Whatever. We trusted Doug was good for the money."

"Doug is dead."

"So, he had insurance, am I right?"

Was there a chance she could make him understand? "The insurance money went to pay off his casino debts. And the business. He took money from the dealership, did you know that? There's nothing left."

"There's got to be something. You got to give us something. An investment gets away, it doesn't make us look good. We have a reputation in the...business community, you might say."

"I can't talk about this now."

"You want I should come to the house?" He smirked when she froze.

Dear Heaven, her children. She had to get rid of this thug before it was time to meet the children. "No. Don't come to the house. I'll pay. I mailed the last check."

"It wasn't enough."

"It's the best I can do."

He shook his head almost regretfully. "See, now, that's

the kind of attitude that's got Uncle Carmine so worried. And then you calling in the police—"

"That wasn't me," she said quickly.

"Whatever. This was a private arrangement. You gonna get other people involved, somebody's gonna get hurt."

This was a nightmare. Frightening. Irrational. She had that sick, helpless feeling that sometimes haunted her in dreams and the same loss of control over her voice.

She forced the words from paralyzed vocal chords. "It won't happen again."

"It better not. Uncle Carmine doesn't like it when people hang up on him. It's like you're going back on your agreement, you know? He thinks you should make, like, a gesture of good faith."

"What kind of gesture?"

"A thousand dollars extra. A month. Until the loan's paid off."

The terms knocked the air from her lungs. He might as well have punched her. "I can't afford that. I can't possibly afford that much."

"I am real sorry to hear you say that. Because if you're not good for the money, you still got to be good for something. I hate to use the word 'example,' but—"

Another voice, male and assured, cut across his. "Hey, buddy, this is my dance. Why don't you beat it?"

Sean. Rachel's heart thudded in her chest. In gladness? In warning?

Bilotti's head swiveled sideways on his very short neck. "D'you mind? The lady and I are having a private conversation."

Sean took his hands out of his pockets. "Yeah, I do mind, actually. The lady made a prior commitment. To me."

"Get lost, wiseass."

"Make me."

"No!" Rachel lurched between them, her hands flattening on Sean's warm chest. What if Bilotti were armed? What if he decided to make an "example" of Sean? "Please, no. He was just leaving. Weren't you leaving, Frank? We can talk later."

Bilotti rocked on his heels to look up into Sean's hard face. "Yeah, sure. Later. I'll be in touch." He tapped one finger between his brows and saluted her before swaggering away.

"You okay?" Sean asked quietly.

She shivered. "Fine."

He reached to take her in his arms, to draw her smoothly against him. "He didn't look like your type."

"He's not."

His thighs brushed hers. They were dancing, she realized, vaguely astonished. He smelled so good, like sundried cotton and himself. He felt so solid, and his hands were warm. The garlanded lights made a crazy halo behind his head as they spun.

"I thought you stood me up," he said.

"No. No, I was just late." She shouldn't be dancing, she thought, resisting the pleasure of his strong lead. She had to get to her children. She had to get them home, where it was safe. "I have to go. Is he watching?"

Sean's mouth quirked. "You're really tough on a guy's ego, you know that? You using me to make him jealous?"

"No. God, no."

"Rachel." His eyes were warm and serious. "What's going on?"

For all his free-and-easy ways, she suspected he wouldn't back down from a fight. And she couldn't live with her conscience if she sent him charging after the thug who'd trashed her living room and threatened her children. "It's nothing. I can't talk about it."

"Uh-uh. Which is it? It's nothing, or you can't talk about it?"

"I don't *want* to talk about it." His hand on her back was warm and sure. How did he know how to dance? "Is he gone?"

Sean looked over her shoulder. "Yeah, he's gone. Listen, I planned on showing you a good time tonight, but if you want that shoulder..."

She did. She wanted everything he offered, kindness and comfort and sex, but she couldn't let herself take any of them. "Thank you. Really."

He lifted an eyebrow. "Thanks, but no thanks?"

"I can handle it."

He pulled her tighter as they turned. "It wouldn't kill you to lean on somebody once in a while."

No, but it could kill him, she thought starkly. She couldn't involve him. She shouldn't even be dancing with him. His body's heat reached through their clothes. Her breasts tingled from brushing contact with his chest.

"Is that what you want?" she asked. "Me confiding in you? Leaning on you? A widow with two kids who lives with her mother?"

"I just want to help."

She shook her head. "For a while, maybe, because you're a nice guy. But you do not want to get sucked into my problems."

Two hours ago Sean would have agreed with her. So why did her dismissal rankle?

For all that she was tall and stacked like an Amazon, she was pliant and graceful in his arms. She shouldn't be hassled by some moron.

"You're pretty quick to write both of us off," he said.

"I'm realistic, that's all. And right now I need to find my kids and go home."

Her kids. Right. He was no part of their tight family unit. But a niggling concern for her prompted him to say, "I'll go with you."

"You don't have to."

"Maybe I will anyway. In case your friend Frankie shows up again."

"I…" He saw the doubt in those big dark eyes and then the acceptance. He wished it didn't make him feel so good. "Thank you."

Her decision made, she didn't waste any more words or time. He caught up with her before she left the dance floor.

Lower lip sticking out at an alarming degree, Lindsey glared at her mother. "We can't leave now. Jackie and I hardly had a chance to do anything. We didn't even get our ice cream."

Rachel looked almost as distressed as her daughter. "Maybe you and Jackie can get together another time." She turned to the pretty black woman standing back with her children, watching the show. "Dee, why don't I call—"

"But Mr. Pittman said he'd take us on the Tilt-A-Whirl!" Lindsey wailed.

Rachel's lips firmed. "Another time."

"There's not going to *be* another time. The fair's almost over."

"I'm sorry, honey, but—"

"You're not sorry at all. You don't want me to have any fun."

"I just need you and Chris to come home now."

Lindsey was hurting. And she reached for words that

would hurt back, hurling them at her mother with a child's accuracy and ruthlessness. "I always have to go where you say. It doesn't matter what I want. You said we had to move. You said we had to live with Grandma. I hate it at Grandma's."

Rachel turned as white as stripped pine.

Remembering her efforts the day they all moved in, the framed flowers over her daughter's bed, Sean felt a surge of protective anger. "Look, your mom has done her damnedest to make a home for you. You should show her the respect she deserves."

"I don't have to listen to you. You're not my father."

"Thank God for that."

"This is not helpful," Rachel said tightly. "Lindsey, we're leaving. Now."

"I won't."

Sean blew an exasperated breath. He didn't need this. But then, neither did her mother. "You've got your marching orders. You want me to carry you out of here?"

"You wouldn't."

It was a challenge. And the MacNeills never backed down from a challenge, even when the would-be opponent was four-foot-eight and wore pink barrettes. "Try me, dollface."

Rachel's friend chuckled. Off to one side with the four boys, her husband watched as the argument got booted from one player to another. Like a damn soccer match. And Rachel was frowning at Sean like he'd just stolen the ball.

But Lindsey, bless her obstinate little heart, wasn't sure he wouldn't carry through on his threat. Rather than risk humiliation in front of her new pal, she shot him a dark look and flounced off with one of those peculiarly feminine noises he usually found kind of cute. Yeah, yeah, you hate me, he thought.

Rachel visibly pulled it together. "Chris, time to go. Dee, thanks."

"Anytime. I'll call you about the girls."

"I'll walk you to your car," Sean said.

Rachel's look was harder to read than her daughter's, but it sure didn't give him a warm, fuzzy feeling inside. "No, thanks. You've done enough already."

"I'll walk you to your car," he repeated. He wasn't leaving her to encounter Friendly Frankie in the parking lot.

She looked from Lindsey's stiff back to her friend's amused face before she gave in. "Fine." Handing him the three-foot-tall spotted dog, she stalked after her daughter.

"Nice to meet you," Sean told the other family.

The woman's dark eyes brightened with appreciation. "Oh, honey, it's been a pleasure."

He lengthened his stride to go after Rachel. He'd never had so much trouble keeping up with a woman. Chris was practically trotting in her wake.

"Take it easy," he said when he reached her side.

"Sorry." She didn't sound sorry. But she shortened her steps.

"Not 'slow down.' I meant, loosen up."

"Easy for you to say."

He wouldn't feel miffed. Hell, she was right. Lindsey wasn't his kid. "You shouldn't get so clutched up about things you can't control."

"That's the problem. There are too many things I can't control right now."

He didn't think they were just talking about Lindsey anymore. "Like your buddy from the bandstand?"

She didn't answer. They walked through a playing field full of cars, the long grass flattened by fair traffic. Behind them, brassy music carried from the Ferris wheel. A chorus of cicadas rose raggedly from the trees.

"Rachel." He didn't know what to say to her. In the MacNeill family, Patrick was the hero, Con the problem solver. Sean was simply "good with his hands." And he didn't fool himself that a rubdown was what Rachel needed now. "What can I do?"

"Nothing." She inhaled sharply. Forced a smile. "There's nothing anyone can do. Don't worry about it."

Good advice. But as Sean watched Rachel unlock her mother's car and load her cranky children into the back seat, he wasn't at all sure he was going to follow it.

Rachel outran her demons, her rubber soles striking the black road in even rhythm. At five-thirty in the morning after a holiday weekend, porch lights were doused. Cars sat idle in dark driveways. Only the birds tuning in the trees offered counterpoint to the chorus in her head.

It's your family you've got to be concerned about.

A thousand dollars extra. A month. Until the loan's paid off.

And Sean's voice, earnest and concerned. *What can I do?*

Nothing.

There's nothing anyone can do.

She pushed herself up the hill, heart pounding. Her breath labored. She counted, timing each quick inhale and slow exhale against her thumping feet. She ran through exhaustion and fear. She ran alone, and the voices kept pace.

By the time she reached the bottom of her mother's driveway, sweat soaked her running bra and the waistband of her shorts. Her legs shook. She bent double, blowing hard.

She had to go in, she reminded herself. She had to face her children and her students, her mother's questions and Bilotti's threats. There was no going back on the road her marriage had forced her along. She could only go forward, one hard step at a time.

Slowly, she straightened, supporting herself with her hands on her thighs. And saw Sean, watching from the top of the drive.

He wore rumpled jeans low on lean hips and an earring. Nothing else. Not even shoes. His broad chest was lightly furred with hair that arrowed down his abdomen. His feet were bare. Judging from his unshaven jaw and finger-combed hair, he hadn't been up that long. But he was drinking. At least, he cradled a tall plastic tumbler in one hand as he watched her.

He started down the driveway, his big bare feet padding carefully over the gravel. She continued to suck in air, willing her heart to slow.

"Here." He offered the full cup.

She hesitated. She was thirsty, but...

"Orange juice. Straight."

"Thank you."

The liquid was cold on her teeth and sweet on her tongue and wet at the back of her throat. She turned the cup to read the lettering on the side. "'Nothing is fool-proof to a fool with the right tools.'" She almost smiled as she handed it back.

"There it is," he said with satisfaction. "You run every morning?"

She wiped her mouth with the heel of her palm. She wished she had more clothes on. She wished he did. "Only when I can't sleep."

"Maybe I should try it."

She felt a pang of sympathy. Of guilt. "Are you having problems sleeping? Is it the couch? Because—"

He shook his head. "It's not the couch, Rachel. It's you."

She felt herself gaping and snapped her mouth shut fast enough to get whiplash. He turned casually away, as if he hadn't said anything out of the ordinary. And maybe he hadn't. Maybe he was just used to delivering come-on lines.

"Coffee's inside," he remarked over his shoulder. "Want a cup?"

Her run had cleared her head of nightmares. But she was tempted by the respite he offered, quiet words and controlled attraction, before she trudged to the house and resumed her "mommy" mantle.

"Coffee would be good."

"You haven't tried my coffee yet. I'm not making any promises."

She didn't want promises. "I'll take my chances," she said.

He'd done more work in the garage, she saw. Secreted away behind the unfinished furniture, in the back corner with her green velvet couch, he'd set up a hot plate and minifridge. An iron lamp glowed from one of his own tables, and a braided rug warmed the concrete floor. She saw books—with a start she recognized Steinbeck's King Arthur and Twain's Huck Finn along with the latest Dick Francis mystery—and a child's drawing stuck with a magnet to the fridge.

"This is...cozy," she said.

"You were expecting beer cans and racing magazines?"

"Am I that predictable?" she asked ruefully.

He shrugged. "Maybe you just think I am." He handed her a maroon mug without a slogan on its side. "I've done the slob bachelor thing. It's not very comfortable after a while."

She sipped the hot coffee with appreciation. "Well, your mother obviously raised you right."

"Oh, yeah. Dad was a marine. Mom was a trauma nurse. He ran a tight ship, and she was into clean hands and hospital corners." He grinned. "Plus, my brothers pounded on me if I didn't do my share."

The story explained his readiness to draft her children when there was work to be done.

"Last night, with Lindsey…" She hesitated. "I'm sorry if I overreacted. I know you were trying to help."

He poured his own coffee and sat on the rug beside the sofa. Even slouching, his head came above her knees. She fought the temptation to reach out, to test the silk of his hair with her fingers. "'S okay. You've got your hands full with that one, though, don't you?"

Rachel stiffened in her daughter's defense. "Lindsey's going through a very difficult time right now."

He raised an eyebrow. "So is her brother. Hell, so are you."

"At her age, she's having more trouble adjusting to a new school. New friends. New everything. And she hasn't really been herself since…since Doug died."

He sat up straighter, dark brows drawing together. "She didn't find him, did she?"

"No." Rachel stared into the depths of her mug, trying not to see. Trying not to remember Doug's gray, distended face lolling against the headrest of the driver's seat as she coughed and cried and searched frantically for the keys. "No. I did."

He swore softly. "I'm sorry."

"Thank you." She clutched her coffee tighter, for warmth.

"In the house?"

"No." She was grateful for that, at least. "He rigged a hose from the exhaust pipe... Doug was a car dealer."

He nodded, to show he knew or to encourage her to continue. She didn't need encouragement. After months of silence, her stifled feelings bubbled out like foam from a can of soda.

"I remember feeling surprised because it was a brand-new Towncar, and Doug was always so careful of things like the upholstery... So stupid. Doug was dead, and I was worried about getting the damn car cleaned."

"Shock," Sean said briefly and sympathetically. "It takes people that way sometimes."

She shuddered. "I'm not a warm person, you know. Not like my mother. Undemonstrative. That's what Doug said."

"I don't think you're cold."

She fixed him with a straight look. "That's sex."

"No. It's the way you are with your kids, your mother. You're a nice woman, Rachel."

His assessment warmed her more than the coffee between her hands. He was being too kind. No matter how seductive she found his comfort, no matter how tempting his understanding, she couldn't let him get the wrong idea about where this relationship was headed. She couldn't let herself get ideas.

"Oh, and you're the expert on women."

"I've known a few."

"But never married."

"No."

"Why not?" she challenged him.

"I was ready to get married once," he said, surprising

her. "I was all of eighteen and ready to be a big man, like my daddy." He took a sip of coffee, cradling the mug in one hand. "Like my brothers."

"I'm sorry." The bitterness in his voice sent her mind whirling through the possibilities. She couldn't imagine any teenage girl turning down Sean MacNeill. "Did she…die?"

He let out a crack of laughter. "Die? God, no."

Her cheeks burned at her mistake. She ducked her head. "I'm sorry, I just thought…"

His eyes were alight with tenderness and amusement. "Thanks. But it wasn't anything like that."

"Then she wasn't ready to get married."

The amusement died. He looked away. "No, she was ready. Just not to me."

"I'm so sorry."

He shrugged. "Yeah, well, it works out that way sometimes. I hear she's happy."

"I think she was stupid."

"Right." His wave encompassed the dim garage. "Look at all she gave up."

"You're very talented."

"I'm very unemployed."

Hadn't she cautioned herself about that very thing? And yet she didn't like hearing him run himself down. "What about your furniture?"

"What about it?"

"Well, you make it. Do you sell it?"

"Some." When she merely waited, he shrugged and added, "There's a guy on the craft show circuit who takes a couple pieces from me. A shop in Boone that sells to tourists."

"How much do they sell?"

"As much as I give them, I guess."

"Have they asked for more?"

He rounded his shoulders, plainly uncomfortable with the shift of the conversation. "Sometimes. Commissions."

She studied this new view of him. "You build custom furniture."

"When I have time."

"Well, you should make time." She sat up, pleased to have a new direction for her thoughts, heartened now that she was encouraging someone else. "You could start your own business."

"It's a hobby."

"It's more than that. You could really make something of it."

He turned his head. His lips curved, but his brown eyes were hard and shrewd. "I'm not one of your students, Rachel. And I won't be one of your projects."

She flushed. "Really? You seem eager enough to make me one of yours."

"One of my what?" His voice had a dangerous edge.

"One of those women you care about as individuals."

"You're too smart to play victim, Rachel. Face it, you didn't come in here to talk about furniture."

Her heart began to slam inside her chest. "I came in for coffee."

"Maybe." He glided to his knees, facing her as she sat on the green velvet couch, his bare chest brushing her thigh. "Or maybe you came in for this."

He leaned forward. His mouth covered hers warmly, surely, before she had a chance to react. Before she could decide how she wanted to react. He tasted like coffee and smelled like sleep, and his skin was hot. Her body tightened. Her eyelids dragged shut as he took the kiss deeper, and then they popped open again.

"No," she said.

His lips cruised up her cheek. He kissed her temple. His tenderness was heartbreakingly sweet and mind-bendingly seductive, but she figured she was on to him now.

"I mean it. If you don't want to talk about it, I understand, but don't distract me with sex."

Sean pulled back. "What are you talking about?"

Her dark eyes were earnest. "As soon as I started to discuss your work, you changed the subject."

He hadn't done that. Sean frowned. At least, he hadn't been aware of doing that. "I did not change the subject."

She flapped away his objection. "Made a pass, then. Same thing."

He was offended at having his lovemaking waved off as a red herring. "The hell it is."

"It's all right," she assured him sincerely. "I understand if you're not ready."

"Beautiful, I am more than ready."

She gave him that schoolteacher look, the one that made him want to kiss her until her eyes crossed. "For sex. But not to talk about something that's obviously important to you."

He stood. She wanted to share? Fine. "So, let's talk. You go first."

Her gaze fell. "I don't know what you mean."

He admired her nerve, but she was a crummy liar. "Who's Frank, Rachel?"

Chapter 8

Rachel's chest caved. She'd prodded Sean to share his hopes and plans with her. She'd needled him to see her as something other than the latest in a string of sexual projects. But now that he'd turned the questioning back on her, she couldn't talk to him.

She closed her eyes in despair. "Oh, God."

"What? What is it?" His voice was deep, concerned. She loved his voice. It sounded more reliable than he looked.

Here was her chance to stumble off the tight little circle of fear and isolation she'd been spinning in like a rat in a wheel since Doug died. And she couldn't do it. Because however important Sean might become, the children came first.

You gonna get other people involved, somebody's gonna get hurt.

Her fingers slid down, tugging at her cheeks, leaving

them drawn and old-looking. "You were right," she said. "Maybe talking isn't such a good idea."

He studied her a moment, bare-chested, thumbs hitched in his belt loops. Two sharp lines dug between his brows. But he asked her lightly, "Does that mean we can have sex now?"

She almost cried. She laughed instead, and some of the worry left his eyes.

"Thank you for your very nice offer," she said. "But—"

"Sounds like no to me."

"I'm concerned about the children, Lindsey especially." That much, at least, wasn't a lie. "I can't do anything that might hurt them."

"Is it just the kids?"

"No. It's everything. I'm muddled enough right now. Sex would confuse things even more."

"We could keep it simple. You. Me. A mattress…"

It was so much less than she wanted. It was more than she could let herself have. She shook her head. "I don't think I could. Keep it simple, I mean."

He inhaled sharply. She watched his chest expand and his muscled stomach contract, and tightened her hands in her lap to keep from touching him.

"I'm supposed to let you go after that?"

She didn't answer.

His breath sighed out. "Yeah. I'm supposed to let you go."

He bent, and his warm hands enclosed her clenched ones as he pulled her to her feet.

"You know where to find me if you change your mind. The offer stays open." He brushed one knuckle down her cheek. The casual tenderness of the gesture almost made her weep. "Both offers, if you want to talk."

She managed to nod. "I'll think about it," she said.

Not that it was a good idea, but he was making it real hard for her to do anything else.

Patrick slammed the tailgate shut, patting the red metal absently, the way he would have patted his plane or his dog. "Got everything?"

"For this trip," Sean said. He came around the back of the truck and stuck out his hand. "Thanks."

"No problem."

They stood in the driveway as eight-year-old Jack retrieved his basketball from the shadow of the barn and drove for the lowered hoop. Sean watched his nephew score in the final seconds of the game for an imaginary stadium of fans.

"Nice shot."

"Yeah." Patrick frowned. "You know, bro, you can still store wood here. Tools, too, if you need to."

"No. You'll need the room for another bicycle soon. The soccer goal. The batting cage. The—"

Patrick raised both hands in uncharacteristic surrender. "All right, all right. Don't remind me."

Sean grinned. "Truth is, I'm outgrowing my space as fast as you're outgrowing yours."

"Thinking of expanding?"

"Could be. I figure as long as I'm unemployed, I might as well give the furniture thing a shot." Sean ran a hand through his hair. This is what came of listening to a woman with a warm heart and big ideas. He looked to the big brother who had been his model all his life. "Dumb idea?"

"No," Patrick said instantly. "I've been wondering when you were going to take the plunge. Talk to Con. He can get you set on the financing."

Sean was mildly stunned. "You two talked about this?"

"You've got the talent. We figured you were just waiting for the right opportunity."

Brianna, an imperious toddler with her father's dark curls and her mother's assessing brown eyes, marched over and threw her arms around her uncle's leg.

"Up," she commanded.

Sean complied, swinging her comfortably onto his shoulders. She shrieked with delight, clutching his hair. Wincing, he carefully shifted her grip.

"She misses having you around," her father observed.

"I miss her, too. She's my best girl."

Patrick lifted an eyebrow. "Yeah? So the new landlady doesn't have anything to do with the change in plans?"

Sean swore. "Somebody's got a big mouth."

"Watch it," Patrick warned. "That's my wife you're talking about."

"And my landlady's got nothing to do with it."

Patrick said nothing, just leaned against the side of the truck and waited.

"It's the daughter," Sean said at last. "Rachel."

"Kate made it sound like you could be serious this time."

"Checking up on me, big brother?"

He shrugged, not denying it.

Brianna drummed her heels against Sean's chest. He flipped her, set her on her feet and watched her run after Jack, disturbing his fantasy game in the middle of a full court press.

"It wouldn't work out," he said.

"Not your type?"

Sean had a sudden uncomfortable vision of Rachel's lush, disciplined body, the humor sparkling at the back of her dark eyes, her sharp tongue and eat-me-up mouth. The man who didn't find her to his type would have to be dead.

"She's a teacher. High school English. Can you see me with a high school English teacher?" He tried to make it sound like a joke.

But his brother wasn't laughing. "It doesn't much matter what I see. The question is, what do you want?"

"She's got kids." Sean threw out the information almost desperately.

Patrick looked out across the lawn, where Jack was attempting to lift Brianna so she could drop a ball through the goal. "Yeah. I know how much you hate kids."

Once upon a time Sean had dreamed of a little girl growing up to call him Daddy. He shook his head. "Hey, yours are great. But the family thing…it's not for me. I'm young yet."

"Thirty next month," his brother observed. "Old enough to take on a wife and kids."

Patrick had always been able to do that, level him with one well-placed punch. When he'd turned thirty, Patrick was already a marine hero running a successful charter flight company. Middle brother Con was a Harvard grad with an office overlooking Federal Street. All Sean had to show for his first thirty years was a brand-new truck and a state-of-the-art table saw.

Never mind. As his teachers had always been quick to point out, Sean wasn't like his brothers. His truck suited him fine. His *life* suited him fine.

"I tried that once, remember? With Trina."

"Wrong woman," Patrick said briefly. "And as I remember it, it wasn't your kid."

Sean moved his shoulders uncomfortably. "That's the

problem. I don't know if I want to go through that again, fall for somebody else's kids. Hell, I don't know if I can.''

Patrick's pilot eyes saw too much. "Then before things go any further, bro, you'd better find out.''

Sean expelled his breath. "Yeah. Guess I'd better.''

He felt like a pervert, hanging around the school, waiting for the kids to come out. He wasn't anybody's daddy. He didn't feel like anybody's daddy, and any minute now one of the nice ladies from one of the family sedans or minivans parked around him was going to rap on the window of his truck and demand to know what he was doing in the car pool line.

Rachel's voice whispered in his head. *I'm concerned about the children, Lindsey especially. I can't do anything that might hurt them.*

Sean set his jaw and stayed. Maybe he wasn't sure exactly what he was doing here, but it had something to do with making things right with Rachel and her children. He'd made an okay start with Rachel. Remembering her warm eyes and her hot mouth and her cool assumption that he could support himself making furniture, he corrected himself. He'd made a great start with Rachel.

But her kids were something else.

Obviously, they were a package deal. He respected that. Admired it. Even envied it, a little, because he'd never had that bond. Oh, his parents loved him. And his brothers had stood with him and by him since he was old enough to stand. But Sean had never had the tie that came from taking care of another person, from being necessary to the well-being and happiness of someone smaller and dependent.

Only once, for three short months. And what a disaster that turned out to be.

Before he got in any deeper with Rachel's kids, he needed to know how he felt about them. He needed to find out how they felt about him, and he needed to do it away from the distracting presence of their mother and the well-meant interference of their grandmother.

The sound of the dismissal bell floated over the parking lot. Doors bumped open. A stream of children poured from the school, building from a trickle to a steady flow. Sean squinted through the windshield, trying to pick out Lindsey's dark ponytail, Chris's narrow shoulders, in the crowd.

The kid in blue? Nah, he was too short. The brunette in purple Keds was too young, and the boy sprinting along the sidewalk wore glasses. Sean drummed his fingers on the steering wheel. Maybe this was another dumb idea. He'd never been all that great at planning.

He glanced idly toward the buses waiting in a yellow line at the side of the school. And there on the sidewalk, a tall girl with dark hair and a thin boy carrying a green backpack were talking to a blocky guy in a gray silk shirt. The carnival guy. Frank.

Sean was out of the truck so fast the driver's side door hung open.

He took five quick strides up the concrete, wading through kids, dodging a boy on a bike. Chris clutched his book bag as he stared at the man looming over them. Lindsey had her chin up and her arms crossed and her brother safe behind her. Sean wanted to hug them. He wanted to snatch them out of harm's way.

He came up to them in time to hear the man say, "...don't have to come to the house to find you."

Sean held his hands away from his sides and said, easy so as not to scare the kids, "Hi, guys. Who's this?"

The man twisted his head toward Sean in a way guaranteed to make him want to knock it off his shoulders. "Friend of the family."

"We don't know him," Lindsey said, looking so much like her mother that Sean wanted to cheer.

"Yeah, well, I knew your pop real well."

The information didn't appear to reassure the two children. It decreased whatever respect Sean still held for Rachel's late husband considerably.

"What do you want?" he asked.

The man spread his hands in a conciliatory gesture as false as a three-dollar bill. "I just wanted to meet the guy's kids."

"You've met them," Sean said. "Now beat it."

"I want to talk to them first."

Sean hitched his thumbs in his front pockets and looked at the children standing on the sidewalk, at Chris's pale face and Lindsey's scowl. Not his kids, he reminded himself. Not his choice. "Do you want to talk to this guy?"

Chris looked at Lindsey. She shook her head.

Sean nodded, satisfied. "Fine. Get in the truck."

Chris's brows pulled together. "Mom said we weren't supposed to accept rides from strangers."

His sister grabbed his hand. "Come *on*, Chris."

She pulled him away, off the curb and toward the truck.

Frank hunched his shoulders and called after them, "See ya, kids. Don't forget to give that message to your mom, now."

Children still ran and chattered along the sidewalk, a bright-colored stream that parted around them.

Sean took a step closer, speaking low. "You stay away from them. You stay away from their mother."

The man's eyes glittered. "Who's gonna make me? You?"

"If I have to. What's your problem? We're on a play-ground, so you feel this need to sound like a bully?"

Frank swore.

Sean shook his head. "I bet the nuns washed your mouth out for that one." He took a step back, keeping an eye on the man's hands. "Stay away from the Fullers."

When he got back into the truck, the guy was still watching him. Lindsey had this look on her face, like she was reserving judgment, and Chris was practically bounc-ing on the bench seat in excitement. It made it hard to shift gears.

Sean pulled out of the parking lot carefully because of the other cars and the walking kids and the crossing guard directing traffic.

"Chris doesn't have a seat belt," Lindsey said in a small voice as they pulled onto the road.

Right. His fully loaded truck wasn't equipped for chil-dren.

"Can you double-buckle?" he asked.

"I guess." She sounded doubtful.

Sean fought to keep his attention on the road as they slipped and scooted and arranged the waist and shoulder straps.

"Okay?" he asked when things settled down again.

She nodded tightly.

"Sure?"

From the corner of his eye, he saw her look away, out the window. She didn't reply. Hell. He reached over, across Chris pressed against his thigh, and patted her knee.

"I'm here, dollface. If you need—" What did he know about what little girls needed? "Anything."

She nodded again.

"This is a cool truck," Chris said. "Can I turn on the radio?"

Sean was amused by the auto worship in his voice. "Yeah, sure."

Rock blasted from the custom speakers. Bass vibrated the cab. Sean adjusted the volume down, so he wouldn't be distracted while he was driving Rachel's children.

It wasn't until they were pulling up the hill to the house that Lindsey spilled what was on her mind. "I wish I knew what was going on."

Sean looked at her, sitting rigid against the cushioned seat. "Yeah. Me, too."

She gave him a brave half smile that would have melted the Grinch. A guy like him—a guy who'd always been susceptible to women—didn't stand a chance.

They pulled into Myra Jordan's driveway. Rachel was waiting on the porch, like she waited every day she didn't pick the children up from school, and when she saw them her face got bright and soft in a way that hit Sean worse than her daughter's smile.

He walked around the front of the truck and then stood back while they ran to her.

"Mom, did you see?" Chris shouted. "Sean brought us home in his truck!"

Lindsey didn't say anything. She slipped her arms around her mother's waist and held on tight. Sean watched the gratitude on Rachel's face slide into question and then fear.

"Is everything all right?" she asked brightly.

Like she could make everything better by pretending. He ambled up the walk, meeting her gaze squarely over the children's heads.

"We have to talk," he said.

Well, damn, thought Rachel.

His jaw was set, his mouth a determined line. The hardness of his expression made him look years older. Intim-

idating, even. Her stomach sank. It was comforting to
think that all that determination was inspired by concern
for her children, but she didn't kid herself.

She was pretty sure they were going to talk. She was
positive she wasn't going to like it. She would have to
lie, and if Sean ever found out, he would hate it. Hate
her.

*You gonna get other people involved, somebody's
gonna get hurt.*

She felt Lindsey pressing against her, thin arms and
smooth hair, and straightened her spine. Not her children.
Her children were not going to get hurt. Even if she'd had
to move them in with her mama, even if she had to scrape
up another thousand dollars a month, even if she had to
look this new, hard Sean straight in the eye and lie her
head off.

She brushed back her daughter's hair and smiled reassurance at her son. "You two go in the house and see
what Grandma has for your snack. I'm going to talk with
Mr. MacNeill a minute."

She waited until the inner door closed behind them before she turned to Sean. He hadn't budged from the bottom of the porch. His usual grin was missing. Her heart
bumped. What had provoked this change in him? And
what was she going to do about it?

"What happened?" she asked quietly.

He hitched his thumbs in his belt loops. "This is going
to take a while. Why don't we go to the shop?"

Trying to test his mood, to find the man she thought
she knew, she teased, "Maybe because every time I pay
you a visit, I wind up plastered all over you?"

"Don't worry. This time I'm keeping my hands to myself until we talk."

"Is that a threat or a bribe?"

His eyes narrowed in appreciation, but he didn't smile. "A promise."

She paused on the last step, clinging to the momentary advantage of height. "You're frightening me," she said lightly.

"Good. Because your kids scared the hell out of me today. Your friend Frankie showed up at their school."

She covered her mouth. "Oh, God."

He cupped her elbow, his warm hand calloused and reassuring.

"It's okay. You raised them right. Lindsey wasn't going anywhere with that guy, and Chris told me he wasn't supposed to accept rides from strangers. They would have been all right."

She didn't believe him. "But you saw them. You gave them a ride home."

"Yeah."

She spoke stiffly, because the alternative was to cry, tears of fear and relief and gratitude. "I appreciate it."

"No problem."

"No, really." She couldn't let her guilt rob him of his due. "*Thank* you."

Her earnestness must have embarrassed him, because he colored under his tan. "They were okay. There were still plenty of people around. They didn't need me."

She walked beside him to the garage, waiting while he fished in his back pocket for the keys.

"They needed someone. I should have been there," she muttered.

He opened the door and gestured her forward. "How could you know?"

Because she'd been warned. She stopped in the empty space bounded by his workbench and his table saw. "I should have known, that's all."

He frowned and flipped on the lights. "Is this Frank following you? Who is he? An ex-boyfriend, a stalker, what?"

"He's a business associate of my husband's."

Sean raised his eyebrows. "Funny business?"

He was too close. "No. Doug...owed him money, that's all."

"And now he's hassling the widow for payment?"

"It's not like that." It was exactly like that. "I'm Doug's executor. We set up a payment schedule."

"So, what's the problem?"

He wouldn't believe her if she said there was no problem—legitimate businessmen did not go around frightening children—so she tried to fob him off with a piece of the truth. "Well, the, uh, business is having a little cash flow problem, and he—"

"He, who? Frank?"

"Yes. Well, no. His uncle," she said, rattled by his persistence. "He works for his uncle. And the uncle wants to increase the payments."

"By how much?"

She didn't see how it could hurt to tell him. The money wasn't the real issue. "An extra thousand a month."

He whistled. "Tough."

Rachel sighed. "Tell me about it. At this rate, I'll be living with my mother until the kids are grown and in college. That's if I can afford college."

"Declare bankruptcy."

"I can't."

"Why not?"

"Because I'm good for the money."

Because if you're not good for the money, Frank's malicious voice reminded her, *you still got to be good for something. I hate to use the word "example," but—*

Sean scowled at her, frustration rolling from him in waves. "The heck you say. Have you called the police?"

She jumped. "No. No police."

"Why not?"

"I really don't see that it's any of your business."

He paced the length of the workshop. "Look, you don't want to sleep with me, fine. That's your decision. You don't want to tell me your problems, fine. That's your business." He stopped in front of her, and his gaze was clear and direct, and his voice was firm and a little angry. "But if somebody's coming after your kids, then I'm making it my business, because they're good kids and I can't help them if you keep me in the dark."

She blinked at him, dazzled by this view of him. Stunned that he saw her children as individuals worthy of rescue and not just as the baggage of a woman he was trying to ease into the sack. It made her want to trust him. It made her want to cry. She could see clearly now that Sean's pirate stubble and earring disguised a caring and honorable man. And Rachel had sold her own honor twelve months ago to protect her children.

"You can't help," she said quietly. "The police can't help. I'm not calling Walter Miller's little brother to tell him I'm being strong-armed by the mob."

"Mother in Heaven." She'd startled him, she saw without any satisfaction. "I thought your husband sold cars. What was he, a drug dealer?"

She'd lost the right to take offense. "No. Wrong addiction. He was a gambler."

"He lost money."

"Lost it, borrowed it, lost some more. And some of the people he lost to weren't very...nice."

"Look, if you're dealing with the mob, you could get the Feds involved. I know somebody—"

Alarm shivered through her. "No. Please, Sean. You have to let me handle this. They warned me. No police involvement of any kind. The one month I was late with a payment, they broke into my home. That time you hung up on Carmine, he sent his nephew to warn me personally. I don't want to think what they'd do if I notified the police."

"Rachel…" He ran a hand through his hair. "You can't fight this on your own. They never picked me for safety patrol, but even I know there are times you've got to tell the teacher. These guys are bullies. And you can't give in to bullies. They just ask for more."

She was afraid he was right. And her fear made her say coolly, "They aren't bullies, exactly. Carmine explained it to me. The Bilottis are businessmen. It's a business deal."

"Uh-huh," Sean said, plainly unconvinced. "Didn't this businessman just screw you for another thousand a month?"

"Well, yes, but—"

"And you're planning on paying it, aren't you?"

She stiffened at the censure in his voice. "To protect my children. Yes."

"So, he wins."

Anger flashed inside her. "This is not about winning or losing."

"Sure, it is. These guys are taking you for everything you've got."

"That is so like a man. Doug never could get up and walk away from a game. Don't you understand? I don't care about anything, as long as they leave my children alone. I'm not afraid of losing."

He came to her then, and took her hands between his big, calloused ones.

"You're wrong," he said quietly. "You are so afraid of losing, you can't win. You need the police."

She flinched from the compassion in his eyes. It was too seductive. "Easy for you to say. No one's threatening *your* children."

He released her hands. "That's right. But I'm not standing around while some goon threatens yours, either. I'm involved now, Rachel, whether you like it or not."

Chapter 9

Sean watched Rachel walk away. Nice view. He wasn't getting any, but that wasn't what made him grind his molars in frustration. For the first time since Trina, he was involved with a woman who wanted less of him than he was prepared to give, and he hated it.

He hated that Rachel didn't trust him to handle things. But then, what had he done to earn her trust? Bringing her kids home had forced her to confide in him. So she would talk to him now, but she wouldn't listen to his advice. She wouldn't accept his help.

He rubbed his unshaven jaw.

Define the problem. His brother Con, the smart one, the one who went to Harvard, said that all the time.

Know your enemy. Patrick said that.

Maybe Sean wasn't the man Rachel needed or wanted, maybe he didn't have Con's brains or Patrick's military know-how, but he figured he had one advantage over his brothers. He waited until the screen door had closed behind Rachel's shapely butt and prickly pride. And then, picking up the phone, he dialed a girl he used to know in Boston.

"Mary Ann O'Riley," came crisply through the receiver.

"Hi, gorgeous."

"Sean MacNeill!" Genuine pleasure lightened the voice on the other end of the line. "I never thought I'd hear from you again."

"It's nice to hear you, too, Mary Ann." He shifted the phone to his other ear. "Listen, something came up down here I was hoping you could help me with."

"The FBI doesn't fix speeding tickets, boyo."

Sean grinned. He'd always liked Mary Ann's sense of humor. But she had a ticklish sense of honor, too, that could be difficult to work around. "Now you know I wouldn't bother you for something like that. This is more a matter of information."

"Sean, we dated for six months and I never could get you to say the three little words that were important to me. What makes you think I'd risk my job telling you anything now?"

"I only need one word, Mary Ann. Just one."

She sniffed, but she didn't hang up. "And what would that be?"

He took a deep breath. "Yes or no?"

"You asking me for a date?"

Hell. "I would love to see you again, but what I really need is more like background information."

"A background check? No way."

"No, not a background check. Just a word, like I said. I'm seeing this woman—"

"And you had to call to tell me."

"This is someone special. And she's in trouble. It

would help me out a lot if I knew how bad the trouble was."

The line hummed. "What kind of trouble?" Mary Ann asked at last.

Sean released his breath. He had her. "That's what I don't know. Family trouble, maybe." He paused. "Maybe one of those big Italian families. Could you tell me that? If I gave you a name? Just yes or no."

"I could do that, I guess," she said slowly. "What's the name?"

"Bilotti. Frank or Carmine."

"That's two names."

"Pick one," Sean said, trusting Mary Ann wouldn't rest until she'd run a check on them both.

"Ha. You owe me, boyo."

"I know it," he said.

"Dinner next time you're in town?"

He hesitated.

"She's that special, huh? The woman you're seeing."

He could have told her no one was that special. Only the thought of Rachel with her little-girl ponytail and her woman's body and her schoolteacher's voice stopped him.

"Could be," he said.

Mary Ann sighed. "All right. I'll see what I can do."

"The Ed Sullivan Show," Rachel said suddenly to Dee-dee Pittman. They were leaving school together, on their way to the teachers' parking lot. "Do you remember that? I must have been about five, but I remember this man running up and down this long table, and he was spinning all these plates up on sticks, and if he didn't get to one in time, everything crashed."

Dee paused on the broad concrete steps. "You are crazy today. Is everything all right? The kids?"

Rachel bit her lip, already regretting her outburst. "Everything's fine. They're fine." And they'd stay fine, too, as long as she got to the elementary school in time. She wasn't risking a repeat of yesterday. "What are you stopping for?"

"Oh, I left my grade book in my desk. I've got to get it. You go on ahead, if you're in such a hurry."

"Thanks. Yes. I'd better."

She hadn't slept, she could barely teach. She'd canceled her after-school help hour so she could pick up her kids. Until Rachel personally told Frank Bilotti she would pay the extra thousand a month, she wasn't taking any chances.

She didn't have his phone number, only the address of a post-office box in Philadelphia. Another plate, spinning out of her control. It was awful, not being able to reach him.

And then she reached the sun-flooded parking lot and saw him leaning against the hood of her mother's car, and that was maybe worse.

She blinked. He didn't go away. He waited, wearing a dark jacket that pulled across his square shoulders and cleaning his nails with a—her stomach flip-flopped—with a knife.

When he saw her, the knife disappeared smoothly inside the jacket. He pushed away from the car. "Hiya, Rachel."

No more "Mrs. Fuller." The omission made her feel as if some indefinable barrier had been crossed.

He looked her up and down. "Guess you got my message."

She unglued her tongue from the roof of her mouth. "Yes." That wasn't enough, she realized. She had to placate him. Get rid of him. "I'll pay the money. The extra thousand a month?"

"That may not do it anymore."

Dismay chilled her. "Excuse me?" she said, like she was asking him to repeat a request to pass the butter.

"I've got to check it with my uncle."

"But...you said—he said—another thousand a month. A gesture of good faith, you called it."

"You got a good memory. But, you know, we made this offer with the understanding that certain private matters stay private. And you—" he wagged one finger at her "—you are not honoring that agreement."

"I am. I haven't called the police."

Bilotti leaned back against the hood of the car, crossing his arms over his chest. "So, what's with the bodyguard?"

Sean. Bilotti was smarting because Sean had made him back down, and now someone—Rachel—would have to pay.

"There is no bodyguard," she said wearily. "He's just a friend."

"Then you be a friend to him. Tell him to stay out of our business."

"I can tell him. I can't guarantee he'll listen."

"You better make sure he does. You don't want another visit like you got in Philly. Because this time when I come around I can't guarantee it'll be when nobody's home."

He pushed closer, so that she could smell his cheap suit and his sweat. Her stomach lurched. She was not going to throw up. She wasn't. She pressed her lips together.

His gaze dropped to her mouth, and lower. "Guess I wouldn't mind paying a visit to your room some night."

Anger flooded her gut, swamped her nausea, almost

drowned her fear. That's it, Rachel thought. She was not standing here like some dumb deer frozen in the headlights while this overgrown delinquent threatened her with rape.

"You won't get the opportunity. I—"

"Rachel?" Deedee Pittman stood at the end of the line of cars, head cocked to one side. "I thought you'd be gone by now."

"I am. I mean, I'm leaving." She fumbled for her keys. "Tell your uncle to call me," she said to Bilotti. "I don't want to see you again."

She enjoyed slamming her car door inches from his hand. She drove off in a cloud of dust and righteous indignation that lasted until she was almost to the children's school. And then she remembered his scowl in her rearview mirror and shivered.

Who would pay for thwarting Frank Bilotti this time?

Rachel stopped in the garage door to watch Sean work. He was completely unselfconscious, utterly absorbed in the grain of the wood and the movement of the plane in his hands, back and forth. Shavings floated to the floor. His arms flexed, his back bent, as he harnessed his cocky energy to work. The steady rasping up and down soothed her.

To her delight, he started singing, chopping the words and rhythm to fit the flow of his labor.

"'My love she won't have me, and I understand. She wants a rich merchant, and I have no land...'"

Her chest tightened. She thought she'd taught herself not to want this way. She was all grown up, with children and debts and responsibilities. But watching Sean, she felt as if she'd wandered into one of the stories she'd loved as a child, stumbled upon the woodcutter in his cottage, the prince in disguise.

"'...and I'll dream of pretty Saro wherever I go.'"

Yearning pierced her heart. But she was too old for fairy tales, and her ogres were all too real.

She swallowed the lump in her throat. "Is this a bad time?"

He straightened easily, awareness of her penetrating his posture. But his grin was open and unaffected and warmed her insides like a fire on a cold night.

"Not if you came out here to call me to dinner," he said.

"Twenty minutes? You have time to change."

"Sounds good," he said, stripping his T-shirt over his head. "I'm starving."

She was, too, and not for Myra Jordan's seven-can casserole. Regret stabbed her. She looked away from his hard, naked stomach, his shadowed navel above the waistband of his jeans.

"After tonight, I think it would be better if you didn't take your meals with us for a while."

Sean lowered his arms, still bound together by his shirt. "Trying to protect me, Rachel? Or yourself?"

She wasn't used to having her motives read so easily. She wasn't sure she liked it. But the humor in his voice and the sympathy in his eyes made it difficult to take offense.

"Maybe I'm trying to protect both of us." She drifted from the doorway, trying not to watch as he tossed his shirt away. Water splashed in the utility sink. From the corner of her eye, she could see the long, smooth muscles of his back and the line of paler skin as he bent over the basin.

To distract herself, she asked, "What are you working on?"

"Table," he answered briefly from behind a towel. "I finished the rocker."

She turned to find it and smiled in pure pleasure.

"It's...perfect." She let her fingers linger over the swell of the back, unable to resist its graceful strength. "It seems almost a shame to sell it."

"I'm not. It's a gift for my brother Con's wife. Val's expecting their first in November."

She was jealous, Rachel realized with a shock. Jealous of the beautiful chair, and the child growing in the unknown woman's body, and the man's love that had put it there. She snatched back her hand.

Sean raised his eyebrows. "It's not that bad a deal. Con paid for materials, and I'm using the plans to build two more. On commission."

Heat crawled in her face. "I wasn't questioning your business judgment."

"Well, you could," Sean said frankly. "But the chair practically sells itself."

"It does," she assured him. "It's beautiful."

The hardness around his mouth faded. "You want to test drive it?"

"No, I..."

He strode to the chair and sat. It rocked gently to receive him. "Come on."

Rachel was a grown woman. A tall, strong woman. Not since her daddy died had anyone invited her to sit on his lap.

She looked at Sean's long-boned thighs. "I'll tip the chair."

"No, you won't. It's solid. If you want to sit, sit."

"I don't know," she said, eying his lap with longing.

"I think you want to."

She met his gaze, and something inside her danced and laughed with the devil dancing in his eyes. "Maybe," she admitted.

"So?" He held his arms wide.

"What the hell," she said, and sat quickly, before she could change her mind.

The chair pitched under her. Sean was laughing, but she didn't mind, because she was laughing, too.

His arms came around her and tugged and coaxed until her upper arm pressed his chest and her hip was snug against his. His skin was cold from the wash water and warm with life, and his chest was rough, and his shoulders were smooth, and his mouth was ripe and firm and smiling. She laced her fingers together to keep them from straying into trouble.

He angled his head. Their faces were very close together. His breath caressed her cheek. "And have you been a good girl?"

She closed her eyes. He smelled wonderful. "I'm beginning to think being good is overrated."

His chest moved with silent laughter. "I've always thought so."

His thigh flexed as he set the chair in motion, tipping her against him. Cradled between the warmth of his chest and the strength of his arms, she exhaled and relaxed. They rocked.

"Why don't you want me to eat with your family anymore?" he asked quietly.

She didn't want to talk about it. Didn't want to think about it. "Because you were right."

"There's a first. Right about what?"

She rubbed her cheek against him, like a cat wanting to be petted. "About bullies."

The arms holding her stiffened. "What happened?"

"Nothing. Well, Frank came to my school today."

"Did he touch you? Talk to you?"

She pushed away the memory of Bilotti crowding her against her car, the unclean touch of his eyes on her mouth, on her breasts. "Nothing happened," she repeated. "But you were right. I think they're going to ask for more money. He's upset about you. 'My bodyguard,' he called you."

"I'll break him," Sean said.

"No. You need to stay away from him. Stay away from us. I don't want you to get hurt because of me."

It was an out, if he wanted one. Only a chump would push himself into someone else's dirty business. Sean tightened his arms around Rachel. And only a wuss would leave her to face this alone.

"I can take care of myself," he said.

"But you can't take care of me. You can't keep a twenty-four-hour watch on my kids."

He already knew he was unqualified to protect her family. But it stung that she thought so, too.

"The police could."

"No police," she insisted tiredly.

"This has to stop somewhere."

"But it wouldn't stop with the police. Even if they made an arrest, I'd have to testify. What if Bilotti's—I don't know—*connections*—decided to shut me up? They could take the children."

Sean shook his head. "Not going to happen. We can make arrangements."

She struggled to sit up. "I'm not dragging them into some witness protection program."

"You wouldn't have to."

"Right. They could just shoot me."

"Rachel, you're not up against the Cosa Nostra here. The Bilottis are strictly small-time. Once you put them away, you're free. It's over."

"You don't know that."

He cleared his throat. "As a matter of fact, I do. I checked with somebody I know. Carmine's a crook, but he's not the mob."

She twisted to see his face. "Somebody you know?"

He decided now was not the time to bring up his old relationship with Mary Ann O'Riley. "With the FBI field office in Boston."

"Oh, God." She pressed her fingers against her mouth; took them away. "You called the FBI."

He continued doggedly. Before she blew up at him, she might as well know the full extent of his interference. "Extortion by wire is a federal crime. There's a field office in Charlotte. I got a name, if you don't want to depend on Officer Friendly for protection."

"Somebody *else* you know?"

"A friend of a friend," he said.

He waited for her to yell. She ought to resent the reminders of his past. He knew she didn't want his well-meant meddling.

"And what would this friend of your friend do?"

"Well, he'd want to talk to you. And then, if you agreed, they'd probably set up a tap on the phone."

She frowned. He wanted to smooth away the double pleat between her brows, kiss the worry from her lower lip.

"It's a risk," she said.

He pulled his thoughts together. "Life's full of risks."

"Too many for me to want another one."

"So, sometimes you have to figure the odds and take

your chances. You want to protect the children? Fine. Here's your opportunity.''

She was on his lap, in his arms, and she might as well have been a million miles away. He could practically hear her sharp mind whirling and whining like a band saw.

"All right."

"All right, what?" he asked cautiously.

She turned her head to look at him, and the trust in her eyes slammed into his midsection like a wrecking ball. "Do what you think is best. Make the call. Set it up."

Her confidence left him winded. Stunned. It didn't help his breathing or his discomfort any when she leaned into him and kissed him. Sweetly, like a girl on her first date or a woman welcoming her husband home. His heart bumped with panic.

"Thank you," she said.

Well, hell. Sean was used to leaping before he looked, going with the flow, living for the moment. It worked well enough. It worked before Rachel. Rachel, straight as ash and strong as oak and constant as the night. Now that she was trusting in him, counting on him, his gut twisted with doubt.

What had he gotten himself into here? What had he gotten *her* into?

Special Agent Lee Gowan arrived on Rachel's doorstep Thursday evening, right before supper.

"If anyone's watching the house, I'm just an old friend dropping by," he'd instructed her during their brief phone conversation on Wednesday. "You can say we need some privacy to catch up, and I'll install the tap then."

So Rachel was almost prepared when she opened the door and a lean blond man who could have stepped off of a recruiting poster promptly kissed her on the cheek and announced, "Rachel! You look great. How are the kids?"

"F-fine," she stammered. Oh, this would never do. She dredged up a smile. "How are you?"

"Great." He waited a moment before prompting her. "Can I come in?"

She flushed and stepped back to admit him. "Of course."

Myra, attracted by the doorbell or the sound of a male voice, drifted from the kitchen. "Well, goodness." Her hands went automatically to her graying blond hair. "Rachel, honey, you didn't tell me we were expecting company."

The agent stepped forward into the hall. "Lee Gowan, ma'am. I'm an old friend of Rachel's."

Myra's eyes widened speculatively. "Really?"

Before her mother could get into where-are-you-from and I-don't-believe-I-know-your-people, Rachel blurted, "Do you mind if we visit in the kitchen, Mama? We have a lot of catching up to do."

Myra's face creased. "But it's so hot in there."

"I don't mind a little heat," Agent Gowan said with a smile that didn't quite reach his blue eyes.

"I'll pour Lee some tea," Rachel said. "And I can finish up the salad while we talk."

"Well, all right." Myra pouted briefly at being deprived of the company of a personable man, but Rachel figured she wasn't able to resist pairing off her daughter. "I guess I'll just go sit on the porch and listen to the bug zapper."

Gowan looked disbelieving as Rachel led the way back to the kitchen. "Was she serious?"

"Of course not. That's Mama being tactful."

Sean came in the back door without knocking. And for

a moment, before Rachel remembered that he could get hurt hanging around her, her heart gave an undisciplined bound and she was really, really glad to see him. For a moment.

She scowled at him. "What are you doing here?"

He grinned back. "I saw the nondescript blue car and your mother out front and figured the feds must be here. Agent Gowan?"

"Lee."

"Sean MacNeill."

They shook, testing grips, sizing each other up.

"You all going to arm wrestle now?" Rachel asked.

Sean laughed.

Agent Gowan pursed his lips. Maybe he figured she was as loony as her mother. "I take it Mrs. Jordan doesn't know why I'm here."

"No. I don't want her involved," Rachel said. She looked pointedly at Sean. "I don't want anyone else involved."

The agent nodded and set a brown paper sack on the kitchen table, as if he'd brought his lunch and was ready to eat now. "I'll get you set up here and then you can leave it to us. This is your mother's house, though, right? Her phone?"

"Yes." Sudden doubt assailed her. "Does it make a difference?"

The agent took something out of the bag. Something small, like a battery. "Not really. I got a bench warrant, just in case."

"In case of what?" Rachel asked sharply.

Agent Gowan unscrewed the earpiece on the phone. He didn't answer, but Rachel had her reply. *In case she changed her mind.*

The next time Bilotti called, everything would be re-

corded. Things were spiraling out of her control. With or
without her cooperation, the investigation would move
forward.

Sean winked at her. "Secret agent stuff."

It was stupid, but she felt comforted.

"All set," Gowan said, hanging up the phone. "Next
time he calls, we'll have ourselves a nice little evidence
tape."

"And then what?" Rachel asked.

Gowan shrugged. "Depends what he says. You can see
me out now."

"What an attractive man," Myra said as the agent
strode back to the uninteresting car pulled into the drive.

"I suppose so," Rachel said. She was still fretting over
the wisdom of calling the police. The FBI. She shivered.

You are so afraid of losing, you can't win.

Sean was right. It was time, past time, to wrest back
control of her life. But she'd never planned on gambling
with her children's safety. She'd never wanted to worry
about Sean's.

"Is he married?" Myra continued.

"I don't think so." She hadn't noticed. Hadn't thought
to ask.

"You should have invited him to stay for dinner."

"Oh, Mama. That ham won't feed more than five. And
Sean's eating with us tonight."

"Yes, but your Mr. Gowan is older. What did you say
he does for a living?"

"I didn't. Mama, you've got to stop trying to fix me
up with anything in pants that comes down the walk. I
told you, I'm not interested in a relationship right now."

No, she just wanted to crawl onto the green velvet
couch with Sean MacNeill one night and beg him to make

her laugh. Beg him to make love to her, to cover her with his broad, hard body and touch her with his big, scarred hands, until she was breathless and mindless and heedless of everything but him.

And that scared her worse than any old tap on her phone.

Chapter 10

The call came at nine that night, when normal people were relaxing, when mothers supervised the last minutes of homework before tucking their children into bed and lovers settled on the couch to unwind and argue amiably over possession of the remote control.

Rachel sat at the kitchen table with a stack of fourth-period personal narratives to grade, two lunch boxes to clean and pack and at least three baskets of laundry to fold and sort. She was wading through Nick Cooper's account of spring break at Myrtle Beach—sixteen years old and the boy was still writing variations on "How I Spent My Summer Vacation"—when the phone rang.

She froze. Stupid, she scolded. Answer it. Answer, before Mama gets it or the kids come down the stairs.

The phone rang again, and she jerked as if the sound was an electric current and she was wired to it. She took a deep breath and made herself move.

Someone, somewhere, was listening to her, recording her. But she felt very cold and alone. "Hello?"

"Mrs. Fuller."

That heavy, formal voice made her grip the receiver tighter. "Yes. Who is this?"

Carmine Bilotti sighed. "You know who this is, Mrs. Fuller. I've got to say, your attitude lately has been a real disappointment to me. I never thought we'd have this kind of problem with a lady like you."

"There's no problem," Rachel said breathlessly.

"That's not what my nephew Frankie tells me. You've got some kind of bodyguard hanging around?"

"A friend."

"A boyfriend?" The voice was reproachful. "Hard to believe poor Doug's been gone only a year."

Rachel closed her eyes. She didn't want to talk about Sean. She didn't want to draw attention to him in any way. "Look, I'm sure you didn't call to talk about my social life."

"Now, that's the truth. Although, you know, it's sort of a reminder. Time passing and all. What I think is, it's time to make final arrangements to take care of our problem."

Final arrangements? Visions of funerals danced in her head. Cold snaked down her spine. "That sounds very…final," she said.

"Funny. What I'm saying is, you can pay off your loan now, in full, and then you and the kids and the boyfriend can make a fresh start."

Bullies always ask for more, Sean had warned her, and he was right. This was much worse than an extra thousand a month. "I don't have the money. You know I don't."

"You have the house."

"I *had* a house."

"The place you're staying in now."

"This is my mother's house."

"And you're her daughter. A loving mother should be willing to help her daughter out."

Not if it meant losing her house, her husband's only legacy. Not at the cost of her own security.

"I won't ask my mother for money," Rachel said fiercely.

"Sure, sure. You don't have to. I bet the place is insured. Against, say...fire?"

For terrible seconds, Rachel let the implication of his words wash over her. Insurance. Doug had killed himself for the life insurance money. Would the Bilottis commit arson to collect again?

"Are you..." The words froze in her throat. Be specific, Agent Gowan had instructed her. She swallowed. "Are you threatening me?"

"Mrs. Fuller." His voice was chiding. "I'm just letting you know how things could be. You want to consider your options."

Her palms were sweating. She was sweating all over, which was odd because she was cold. So cold. "I have no options."

"Sunday," he said. "That gives you enough time to get to the bank but not enough to do anything foolish. Give me your number, and I'll be in touch."

She struggled to make sense of his request. Her brain felt sluggish. "My number? I'm here."

"You got a cell phone? Believe me, you don't want to miss this call."

She did have a mobile phone, in case the children ever needed to reach her. Automatically, she gave him the number.

"Right, then. The full amount, in cash, on Sunday. I'll call."

"But—"

"Consider your options, Mrs. Fuller. You have a lot to lose." He hung up.

Rachel sagged against the wall, still clutching the receiver. She wanted to whimper. She wanted to cry and be comforted in strong, warm arms. She wanted Sean.

Not his problem, she reminded herself sharply.

The phone was tapped. Extortion by wire was a federal crime. Sean had said so. All she had to do was hold on and wait for Agent Gowan to get in touch with her, and her children and her mother would be safe and her life could go back to normal.

Consider your options, Mrs. Fuller.

She began to shake.

From the living room TV, a blast of music cued the cut to commercial. Myra Jordan chirped, "Rachel? Who was that on the phone?"

"Nobody, Mama."

She had to get out of here. She would not go running across the backyard to Sean. She pushed away from the wall, her gaze skidding from the stacks of paper and piles of laundry to her running shoes bundled into the corner by the door.

Escape.

She grabbed them. On the edge of her seat, she tied her shoes, her fingers trembling. The TV chattered from the other room.

Grateful for whatever program had claimed her mother's attention, Rachel called, "I'm going out for a while. To clear my head."

"All right, dear," Myra answered.

Rachel ran.

She did about a mile before her blood finally warmed, before her muscles loosened and her heartbeat regulated. *Control.* She congratulated herself. This was what she needed. She'd taken up running again after Doug died to make herself fit, to keep herself strong, to regain control over a tiny portion of her life. It was quicker and a whole lot cheaper than paying some therapist to tell her she was under stress. For heaven's sake, she knew that.

She ran. She was stretching into a comfortable rhythm when she noticed the headlights behind her.

She was suddenly, uncomfortably, aware of her isolation.

Don't overreact. It was just some factory worker coming off his shift or a teenager driving home from a friend's or...who else would be on a back country road at almost ten o'clock at night?

Rachel moved even farther onto the verge and slowed her pace. The car behind her slowed, too. Was there something familiar about the rumble of that motor?

She stumbled. Her pulse roared in her ears. There were no lights on this road, only the dim glow of a moon she could no longer see in the glare of the headlights. She would not stop. She would not turn around. She would not panic unless the car behind her stopped and someone got out.

Gravel crunched. The car behind her stopped. She heard a door slam.

Oh, God. She sprinted ahead, afraid to run for the trees on either side. Teacher's Body Found In Woods, her mental headline shrieked.

Feet pounded behind her. A deep voice shouted. She frowned in recognition. Maybe—?

But before she could think or react, a hand, hard and bruising, slipped down her arm and grabbed her elbow.

She tried to twist away, but it was too strong and she was spent. Catching her with his other arm, her attacker pulled her back into his hot, solid body. With a desperate cry, she whirled, driving her elbow as hard as she could at his midsection.

"Ow! Damn."

Sean.

She stopped struggling, peering at his face in the long shadows cast by the headlights.

"You nearly broke my ribs," he complained.

"You scared me," she accused.

"Well, you scared me. Your mother said you'd gone out. What if I'd been a bad guy?"

Her heart still pounded. She raised her eyebrows. "I guess I would have nearly broken your ribs."

He expressed his opinion of that in two short words.

Rachel almost smiled.

"Sweet Mother in Heaven, don't you realize Friendly Frank is out there somewhere?"

He was yelling at her the way she'd yelled at Chris when he was three years old and ran into the street. "Naturally, I realize—"

"It was a stupid thing to do. You've got to take care of yourself."

She was trying. "I do."

"You're not doing a very good job."

"And I suppose you could do better?"

"I could hardly do worse. Myra told me you got a call. Was it Bilotti?"

She put up her chin. "What if it was?"

"Why the hell didn't you come to me?"

"I…" What could she possibly say? "I thought about it."

"Well, that's great." He released her to run a hand through his long hair. "That is just great."

"I don't understand why you're so angry with me. It's not your problem."

"Maybe I'd like it to be."

"No, you wouldn't," she said wearily. "Nobody would. Even *I* don't want my problems."

He squinted at her in the glare of the headlights. "Rachel…"

"Doug didn't want them, either." She sucked in a painful breath. "Which explains, I guess, why he killed himself."

Sean swore and jerked her to him abruptly, wrapping her in his hard, strong arms. His heart thudded against her palms. His breath stirred her hair. "What the hell are you doing to me, Rachel? What am I going to do with you?"

His tenderness broke her when his anger could not. She felt tears burning the back of her throat and gulped aggressively.

"I'm not crying," she mumbled into his shirt.

"You can. You should."

"No. I look ugly when I cry."

"Says who?"

"I do. Little girls, pretty girls, cry pretty little tears. My face gets ugly and red."

"You mean, you look like a human being instead of a doll."

She shuddered against him. He threaded his fingers through the hair near her scalp. Combing it back, he kissed her temple and the space between her brows and the bridge of her nose. His breath was warm. His lips were firm. He kissed her cheekbone and her wet lashes.

"Real tears," he said. "You're one of the realest people I've ever known. And you can cry in my arms anytime.''

She knew better than to believe him. It hurt too much. "Anytime until you leave."

"What do you want, Rachel?" he asked quietly. "Promises?"

When had promises ever done her any good? Her father's promises, her mother's, Doug's?

I'll be there for you, Rachel.

It will be different this time, Rachel.

It's nothing to worry about, Rachel.

"I don't know," she said. "I haven't had much luck with promises. What are you offering?"

"I don't know." After a long minute his arms tightened and then he let her go. "Let's figure it out in the truck. I don't want you sideswiped by some Bubba who shouldn't be out after dark."

She nodded, too tired to resist his seductive concern any longer. Too aware she was becoming dangerously dependent on his support.

They walked back to the truck, its motor still running. He opened her door. His courtesy no longer surprised her. It wasn't an anachronism or an act, but a measure of his genuine kindness. That didn't mean she should take advantage of it. Of him.

He swung in beside her and switched gears. She tilted her forehead against the cool glass, watching her breath condense, a silver circle of fog on the window. The night rushed by behind it, blank and dark. Sean drove with his window down and his elbow propped on the door, and after a while the wind in the cab faded the marks of her breath.

Rachel sat up. "This isn't the way home."

"I know."

"Where are you going?"

His teeth gleamed in a pirate's smile. "Joyriding."

"I need to get back. I still have papers to—"

"You need this more. I need this."

Silenced, she sat as he drove past houses put up in what used to be pastures. A lone dog barked a warning from a farmhouse. The trees waved dark arms against a deep sky.

Sean slowed at a deserted intersection, and the truck bounced off the road.

"Where are we?" she asked.

"Logging road."

"Aren't those closed to the public?"

He shrugged. "I know a way past the gate."

The truck lurched down a grassy alley along a string of electric poles. The moon filtered dimly through the trees. Rachel balanced herself with one hand on the dashboard. She really ought to protest that what they were doing was foolish. Illegal. She was a good daughter, a widowed mother of two, a high school English teacher charged with setting her students an appropriate example…and what had being a Nice Girl ever gotten her but a mother who abdicated her responsibilities and a husband who gambled and a small-time racketeer who had no qualms threatening her home and her children?

She looked at Sean, his face hard in the green light of the dashboard, his hands easy on the wheel. A spark of excitement flared beneath her ribs. She bit her lip.

"We're trespassing. What if we get caught?"

"You don't fell trees in the dark, beautiful. The guys clear out of here by four, four-thirty. I know, I drink with most of them."

The spark kindled, warming her with possibilities. "So, we're just going to…park?"

The truck jounced onto a rutted track. Sean raised one

eyebrow. "You think I drove out here so we could have sex with your heels on the dashboard and the gearshift in the way?"

She was abashed. "Probably not."

"There's something I want to show you."

The trees ended abruptly. The sky arched overhead. Rachel stared out the windshield at a clearing pocked with great muddy holes and littered with roots and picketed with uneven stumps. A few bare trees stood like pilings. Heavy equipment humped in the shadows, dinosaur-sized and shaped, its bright yellow faded to gray by night. It looked like a bomb site or a scene from an alien planet or a landscape ravaged by flood.

"You drove out here to show me this?"

He eased the truck forward onto the barren clearing. "Yeah."

"It's empty."

Wasted. Desolate. She was disappointed, worse than disappointed, her little flicker of sexual excitement snuffed right out by his obvious disinterest. She felt as dreary as the grim terrain around them.

"That's because you're not looking at it the right way yet," Sean said. He parked the truck and walked around to her side, opening the door. "Come on."

She hesitated.

He held out his hand for her, impatience edging his voice. "Come on."

Disdaining his help, she jumped from the truck and then almost wobbled into him as she landed on uneven footing. He steadied her with hands under both elbows. It was the perfect opportunity for a man with sex on his mind to hold her close and gaze into her eyes and murmur something suggestive about knocking her off her feet.

Sean released her arms and walked around to the back of the truck.

So, all right, he didn't have sex on his mind. He'd made that plain. Rachel sighed and followed him.

The tailgate creaked down. Sean reached for the folded moving pad he used to protect his furniture and shook it out and spread it, providing her with a nice view of his muscled forearms and well-defined back, and then vaulted into the back of the truck. Crouching, he extended his hand to her. This time she took it.

She scrambled up.

"Lie down," he commanded.

She ignored the spurt of her pulse. He wasn't thinking about sex. Was he? "Why?"

His smile gleamed again. "Trust me."

She yearned for him with an ache so sharp she almost gasped. She coughed instead. "Do you know how many high school girls have regretted falling for that line?"

"I never kept count," he said, deadpan, and chuckled at her frosty look. "Pretty Rachel. Please?"

She grumbled. "All right." She flopped gracelessly onto her back. The stars wheeled overhead. "Now what?"

"Close your eyes."

She was afraid to accuse him of setting her up because she was so depressingly certain he wasn't. She shut her eyes.

His voice reached out in the darkness. "What do you smell?"

She started. "I… Woods?"

His warm hand took hers. He squeezed encouragingly. "Pine tar," he said. "Juniper. Oak. Cedar in the underbrush."

She couldn't distinguish the varieties the way he did, but his deep voice enveloped her as easily as his fingers wrapped her hand. She wanted to protest: you didn't spread a blanket in the woods with a gorgeous hunk of twenty-something to talk about trees. But he didn't want to do anything else. And so she let his words wash over her, sink into her, while the metal ridges struck through the pad beneath her and the warm air brushed her knees. Sensitized to the night's undertones, she lay very still and absorbed them, the sharp scent of pine, the earthy smell of decomposing leaves.

"It smells like fall to me."

"That's tannin from the cut oak."

"It smells...sad. All those dead trees."

"Sad? No. It's giving new life to the wood in tables and chairs. Houses. Cradles. The trick is doing it right, keeping the soul in the work. We live with too much plastic."

"You're an artist," she observed softly.

"Me?" He sounded embarrassed. "Nah. I'm just some Joe Blow carpenter."

But this time he was wrong. He was so much more. The clues to his nature were in his work, in the way he brought purpose and hope where she saw devastation. Flat on her back in the bed of his truck, she marveled at the big, scarred hand pressing hers, the power of bone and sinew, the pulse of life, the connection forged between them.

She *had* needed this. Needed the scent of the earth and the kiss of the air to put her fears and problems in perspective. Needed the strength and laughter of the man beside her to restock her depleted heart.

"Now open your eyes," he whispered.

She did, and saw the stars, brilliant in the gray velvet sky. The reflected glow of the city hovered above the tree line.

What are you offering? she had asked him. Here was her answer. Peace. Friendship. Stars and shared confidences. All good things. But not enough. Not for her. Not anymore. She was tired of being the nice girl, of waiting for him to seduce her, of waiting for things to be offered instead of taking what she wanted.

She was thirty-four years old and stargazing wasn't enough.

Well, hell. Sean stared up at the cold and brilliant sky and tried real hard not to think about the warm and breathing woman lying next to him.

He was going to be noble if it killed him. Which, he figured, it probably would. He was already dying and she didn't have a clue, stretched out beside him with her runner's knees in the air, the hem of her shorts sliding down to expose her strong, smooth thighs, and her well-shaped hand trusting in his.

She was fine and real and vulnerable, and she had enough on her mind right now without worrying about him jumping her bones.

Too bad he couldn't think of anything else.

He drew in a careful breath. A better man wouldn't notice how the scent of her reached through the darkness. Patrick would think about honor and Con would do tax tables or something in his head. Sean could only curse himself for a fool and ache.

He heard her sigh and felt her shift and tried not to imagine how it would feel to have her sighing and shifting under him. She let go of his hand and turned onto her side, toward him. If he looked—and of course he looked, he was only human—he could see the dark strands of her ponytail snaking across the sweet inside curve of her arm, black on white, like a written invitation. Her smooth, bare knees nudged his thigh.

That was it. He was going to hell.

He was there already, burning up with lust when she needed his patience and protection. Desperately, he tried to think himself out of his body, focusing on the cold and distant sky.

And then she lifted up on her elbow, and her face replaced the stars, and she kissed him fully, warmly, on the mouth.

Desire slammed into him. Her mouth was slick. Her lush breasts flattened on his arm. He imagined them filling his hands, peaking against his palms, and he curled off the truck bed, his arms going around her, one hand already fisting in her hair.

She came right back at him, genuine and generous. Hungry. Hot. His hands moved on her blindly, pulling her top free of the waistband of her shorts, following the curve of her rib cage, seeking the warm damp skin beneath.

She shuddered, murmured, moved. His libido grew teeth like an industrial saw, sharp enough to chew through masonry, to make sawdust of his good intentions.

He shook his head, trying to think through the buzz. "Rachel."

Her warm mouth fastened on his neck. He hoped she would forgive him for what he was about to do, because he was pretty sure he would never forgive himself.

"Rachel...stop."

She lifted her head. Her lips were full and wet and curved. "The gearshift's in the way?"

Despite his frustration, he laughed. "No, that's me."

"It feels wonderful. You feel wonderful."

"Sweet Heaven, Rachel." As prayers go, it was inadequate but sincere. He definitely needed the help of the angels here. "We can't do this."

She pulled back with an honest look that cut straight to his heart. "You don't want to?" she asked quietly.

Hey, the angels wouldn't want him to lie, would they? "No, I want to. I don't think we should."

She bit her lip. "Don't tell me you haven't done this before."

"More often than you," he muttered. "I don't want you to get hurt."

Her eyes were warm with relief and understanding and something else he couldn't read in the darkness. "That's very virtuous of you."

"No." He was embarrassed. Insulted. "It's just... You're just in a tight place right now. I don't want to take advantage."

She nodded thoughtfully. "Thank you. How would it be if you just lie there and I take advantage of you?"

The air left his lungs in a rush. Images of Rachel using him for her pleasure, for his, ignited in his brain. And before he could twist his thoughts or his tongue into objections, she poured over him like fire, and the reality of her burned through his imaginings.

She covered him, her long, smooth legs tangling with his, her strong, supple back arching under his hands, her breasts rubbing his chest. She was liquid heat, her fingers dragging at him, stroking, stoking. Heat blurred his brain as her mouth fastened on his.

He wanted to show her tenderness. Technique. Finesse.

She didn't wait. Her mouth was avid. Her hands went to the button on his jeans. His body lurched in unbelieving pleasure.

Capturing her hands, he yanked them to either side of his hips, fighting for control. She tugged at his jeans, wriggling above him, and something inside him snapped.

He rolled with her, forcing her under him, holding her

still with the weight of his body. Her thighs parted to cradle him, and he could feel the lush, moist heat of her straining against him. His muscles contracted. He wanted her with a desperation that bordered on pain, wanted to take and take.

He was used to looking out for his own pleasure, for his partner's. Always before he could slow things down or speed things up to make it happen. And now all he could focus on was stripping her of her clothes and pushing into her tight, hot body and pumping to completion. His lack of control—his lack of choice—scared him.

He thrust against her crudely, making her feel the pulsing demand of his body.

"What do you want, Rachel? This?"

She met his gaze, her eyes honest and unafraid in the dim moonlight. Her mouth was swollen. "You. I want you."

Her words burst his control. He went crazy. He pulled at her shorts, shoved at his jeans. Even in his madness, he was aware that she helped him, or tried to help him, their hands sliding and colliding in the tangle of their clothes, the press of their bodies.

He growled. "Let me."

She arched. "Hurry."

His hands were shaking so bad he could barely lift his wallet, but he managed to find and use the condom. He didn't know if it was habit or concern for her, but he managed that much.

She moved restlessly. Reached for him. Her short schoolteacher's nails dug into his skin. He held her down, pushed her open. He started giving it to her, fast and hard, and these soft, beautiful, animal sounds tore from her throat as her strong arms gripped him and her smooth thighs wrapped him and her inner muscles kneaded him. Willing. Eager. His.

He levered himself on his elbows and yanked up on her top, on her bra, so that her breasts surged free, pale in the moonlight. Her nipples were dark and tight. He sucked on them hard and felt her peak, felt her shudder and come apart in his arms. She was crying out, and he felt an answering shout swell inside him, in his chest and in his soul. It filled him until it was too much to contain. Too much to control. Too much. Like a wave it took him, and every time he thought to ride it in, another, bigger wave rushed in and knocked him down. He was drowning in her, drowning in her moans and the wet, hot clasp of her body and her scent, until the final, biggest wave tore through him, and he emptied himself into her with a jerk and a roar.

From a tall branch high above them, a night bird cried and launched into the night.

Chapter 11

Crushed between the cold, flat moving pad at her back and the hot, hard weight of Sean along her chest and belly and thighs, Rachel had never felt more free. Her blood still surged. Her pulse still rioted. Her body shivered with lovely, charged aftershocks.

She moistened her lips and found her voice with effort. "That was…"

The body above hers stiffened. "Too rough?"

"I was going to say, incredible."

He relaxed on her, all that wonderful heat and weight pressing, pinning her down. "Yeah, that about sums it up. Are you always…"

"A screamer?" she asked dryly. "No."

His laughter was a breath on the side of her face, a rumble low against her stomach. It felt fantastic. And then his muscles collected and he started to lever away. "We did get pretty wild."

She missed the pressure of skin on skin, resented even

the slightest loss of contact. She wanted him on her. In her. But she let him shift to the side, feeling the drag of his jeans as he rolled. He hadn't even undressed. Amazing.

"I suppose it could have been the primeval setting," she said uncertainly. Did he want distance? Her legs were cold.

But he gathered her against his shoulder, fitting her snugly into his warm side. "Honey, this isn't Jungle Land. I don't think it was the setting, unless the truck did it for you. High CDI factor in trucks."

She sighed with contentment. "CDI factor?"

"Chicks Dig It." He laughed when she bit his shoulder, and stroked a hand down her back. "Are you okay?" His voice was deeper. Softer.

She wriggled against him. "Oh, yes."

He exhaled, still holding her close. "Good."

They lay there quietly. The night hummed around them. The stars pulsed overhead.

Sean spoke. "Might have been an adrenaline thing."

A tendril of doubt uncurled in Rachel's chest. Did he mean that this incredible explosion between them, this lightness of being, this newfound freedom, wasn't him? Wasn't her? *Don't take it too seriously.*

"You mean, like stress release?" she asked cautiously.

His shoulder moved beneath her cheek as he shrugged. "It's one explanation. We could try it again now that you're relaxed. I'm willing."

"That's very generous of you."

"Well, in the interests of science…"

"Or it could have been that I haven't had sex in over a year," Rachel said sharply. Too sharply, she thought the instant the words left her mouth.

The hand stroking her back stilled. He tangled his fingers in her hair and raised her head so he could study her face in the moonlight. His gaze was direct and hard.

"Maybe the long dry spell explains it for you, beautiful. But that doesn't account for my little out-of-body experience, all right?"

She was reassured. "It was…okay?"

"You blew my mind," he said honestly. "You wrecked my control. You want a testimonial?"

She kissed his shoulder. "Not a testimonial, no. Maybe a repeat performance?"

His breath whooshed out. In amusement? The hand in her hair shifted its grip. "I'm willing," he said again, and brought her mouth down to his.

His breath was hot. He licked inside her mouth, and she felt herself softening, melting down. The overwhelming suddenness of her response staggered her. Frightened her. She wanted abandon, and she was in thrall to him, to the need he created in her quickening heart and womb.

She made a grab for the old Rachel, the Rachel who never lost herself in the back of a truck with a beautiful man. "I don't know. Do we have time?"

He laughed, actually laughed at her. "I'll be quick," he promised.

And he was willing. How willing, she could feel against her thigh. He was rigid and silky hot, and her thighs went lax even as she tightened deep inside. His hands were hard. He felt so good, so solid and warm, and she wanted him. He sprawled her limbs and made her climb on top this time, so he could watch. His eyes were glittering slits.

She shivered. He pulled her top over her head, leaving her briefly blind and confused, and then his hands were all over her, on her breasts, between her legs. Desire bowed her back as he filled his palms with her and held her hips and moved her up and down, urging her on. It was shameless. It was exciting. And she took him, all of him, everything he had to offer, the freedom and the power and the hot, lovely slide of his body.

She came fast, shuddering as he filled her. He didn't let her go. He held her, thrusting up, again, again, before his release racked them both and he gripped her tight with his big, hard hands and gasped into her hair. He let her collapse then, pulling her onto his broad, damp chest. She was still quaking inside.

And as the stars wheeled and the night settled around them, she knew it wasn't the setting or the adrenaline or even her long celibacy that explained her response.

It was Sean.

He was all her best and baddest dreams come true, all the things she'd never allowed herself to have and to be. She touched his chest, indulging in the feel of warm muscle and rough hair under her fingertips. But she was attracted to more than his to-die-for body and color-outside-the-lines attitude. He was decent and hardworking and kind. She nuzzled her face against his damp shoulder. Just look at the way he'd dragged her out here to comfort her.

Was that why he'd made love to her, too? Let her make love to him? Out of kindness?

Her blood cooled. She squirmed.

Be a grown-up, she instructed herself. If that *was* Sean's strategy, it had worked, damn it. She was grateful, more than grateful, for his comfort and his laughter. For the temporary freedom and the temporary sex. And she wasn't about to repay him for his gifts by reading any more into the situation or clinging to him now.

He deserved better. Her pride demanded more.

So she waited until she had herself and her voice under control, and then raised her head and said—*Lightly,* she cautioned herself, *lightly*—"You were right. That *was* quick."

There was a heartbeat pause before he asked lazily, "Complaints, already?"

"No. None at all. I have to get back."

"Right."

He sat up with her, supporting her. Without fuss or hurry, he adjusted his own clothes and helped her find her underwear. Struggling to jam on her shoes in near-darkness, Rachel wondered at his lack of awkwardness.

He must have done this many times before.

It was a sobering thought to carry back home along the dark and rutted road. She pressed her hands together in her lap as if she could hold on to that instant of freedom under the stars, that illusory closeness, that moment when her soul flew. By the time they pulled into the driveway, her palms were damp with sweat.

His headlights swept the garage door in great white arcs.

"You want me to come in with you?" he asked quietly.

Like this was a date, and he had to meet her mama.

Rachel imagined Myra looking up from the news, busy eyes bright with interest as she examined Rachel's clothes and Sean's hair. She shivered.

"No. Thanks for the ride," she added politely and then winced. It sounded as if she was thanking him for...for... If he laughed, she would hit him.

"I'll see you tomorrow, then." His voice was bland.

"Tomorrow."

Thoughts of what faced her the following morning swept in on her, more oppressive than the baskets of un-folded laundry and pile of ungraded papers that waited for her in the kitchen. Bilotti's threats, Gowan's instructions, her worries for her children... Hemmed by responsibilities and pressed by fear, she could barely breathe.

She got out of the truck. and she didn't look back.

Great sex. No strings.

It really ticked him off.

Sean fed another board into the saw, taking satisfaction in the blade's bad-tempered howl. For all his reputation and experience, he didn't go for wham-bam-thank-you-ma'am encounters. Well, not often. And not lately. He really did see the women he liked as individuals, delightful in their differing shapes and ways and personalities. He didn't even go to bed with some of them.

Golden sawdust flew into the air. Sean propelled the board, his movements powered by an unfamiliar blend of virtue and steam. So if Rachel Fuller thought she could give him the best sex of his life and then act as though they had nothing in common and no possible future, she was...

Probably right.

Damn. He lifted the board to set it out of the way, against the wall, and shut off the saw. He had no business taking up with a woman who required stable hours and a steady paycheck from her man, even if she did make his heart beat like a drum. He had no desire to play daddy to her appealing brats, even if Chris did need someone to show him how to fold a pocketknife and Lindsey deserved a safe adult to practice her wiles on. They would only be hurt when he moved on. He would be hurt.

After Trina, he never wanted to be responsible for anyone again. So why the hell had he put them all at risk by getting involved now?

Tugging off his powdered goggles, he scowled toward

the house. And saw Agent Gowan's nondescript blue car pulled up at the curb outside.

The feds were here, and Rachel hadn't called him.

The observation lit Sean's uneasy temper like a match to kindling. He was tired of waiting by the phone like a lovesick teenager hoping for an invitation to the prom. Like some girl he was letting down easy. The thought made him wince. Clamping his jaw, he stomped toward the back door.

Through the screen he could hear voices, Lee Gowan's and Rachel's. She was speaking in that cool school-teacher's tone he admired, the one that made him want to put his hands on her just to see if he could ruffle her composure.

"...don't want my children in danger. What if he changes his mind and comes here?"

"Won't happen. Don't worry about it. Sounds to me like Bilotti wants to avoid involving your boarder or any-one else. Your kids are safe enough."

And what about Rachel? Sean wanted to demand. What about her safety?

"But can't you pick him up now?" she asked. "Ex-tortion by wire is a crime, you said."

Agent Gowan cleared his throat. "The prosecuting at-torney would really like us to go for the drop at this point, ma'am. To ensure a conviction."

"The only thing I want to ensure is that Bilotti doesn't get anywhere near my children."

"For how long?" Sean, listening at the door, tensed at Gowan's challenging tone. "You want to make sure this guy's locked up for good, Mrs. Fuller."

"But my children—"

"Why don't you see if you can get them away for the

next couple of days? Do you have relatives they could stay with?''

"I'm already staying with my mother, Agent Gowan," Rachel said wearily.

Sean had heard enough. He respected Rachel's determination to safeguard her children, but he was annoyed anyway. With her, for not caring more about herself, with Gowan, for not insisting on her safety, with himself, for not being in a position to do anything about it.

Well, maybe he had no right to protect her, but he could help her protect her children.

"Somewhere else?" Gowan was saying. "Someplace they all could go, maybe?"

"Yeah." Sean pushed open the door. They both looked up in surprise. "My brother Patrick's place. He's forty minutes away. That takes them out of harm's way, but they'd still be close enough for you to keep tabs on them."

"That's settled, then," Gowan said with evident relief.

"It is not," Rachel snapped. "I can't let you put your brother's family in danger."

Sean was absurdly proud of her concern, her stubborn spirit. He turned to the agent. "Would they be in danger?"

"I don't see why. As far as we know, Bilotti's acting on his own down here. He can't pick up the drop and search for the children at the same time."

Sean shrugged. "So, we're good to go."

"But the inconvenience," Rachel protested. "Why would your brother do this for us?"

"Because I'm asking him for help."

Her dark eyes were genuinely bewildered. "But... why?"

"Because you won't. Jeez, Rachel, what kind of life

have you had, that you can't believe in a little help when it's offered?''

Gowan scowled. ''Maybe you folks want to continue this discussion another time.''

''Fine.'' Sean dragged out a chair and straddled it, ignoring Gowan's narrowed eyes. ''So, did our buddy Carmine set a time and place yet?''

He waited for Rachel to tell him to get lost. But all she said was, ''Sunday. I have to come up with the money by Sunday.''

''You'll need to make a decision soon,'' the federal man said. ''Banks are closed tomorrow.''

She made a hopeless gesture with one hand. ''It hardly matters. I don't have it.''

''We can provide you with a decoy bag, Mrs. Fuller. It will look real enough. We'll place the money pack inside that, like a hundred twenties bundled together, to hold your transmitter in case Bilotti gets away from us at the drop. And of course you'll be wired.''

''No wire,'' Sean objected.

''Why not?'' Rachel said.

''It's not your decision,'' Gowan said.

Sean set his jaw. ''Look, I've met this bozo. I'm not giving him any excuse to tear off her blouse. No wire.''

Gowan looked at Rachel. She moistened her lips. ''No wire,'' she agreed.

Relief spread through Sean.

Gowan nodded reluctantly. ''Okay. We'll tap the bag and the car. You'll be able to speak into the car transmitter to keep us apprised of your situation. Once Bilotti calls back with a location, I've got a team of agents I can bring in to apprehend him at the site and block the exit roads.''

''What about her? Who's protecting her?''

''Look, I understand your concern. But it's very possible Bilotti won't even try to pick up the money until she's left the scene.''

"And if he wants her to hand it over personally?"

"We'll be there. Once we're in position, we'll have two angles on Mrs. Fuller at all times." Gowan's chair scraped the floor as he stood. "We do know what we're doing. There's no reason for her to worry. And there's absolutely no need for anybody to play cowboy. You follow me?"

"Thank you, Lee, that was very clear." Rachel stood, too, and offered him her hand. "I appreciate you coming by."

The agent held on to her a little longer than Sean figured was necessary. "We're monitoring your calls. When Bilotti gets in touch with you, we'll know."

"Thank you."

She walked him to the front door. Sean stayed stubbornly where he was, in possession of Rachel's kitchen. As far as he could tell, the agent was as straight-arrow as they came. A regular Boy Scout. It didn't make Rachel's dependence on him any easier to take.

She came back, smiling mouth and tired eyes in a pale face, looking so beautiful Sean's chest hurt. He wanted to tuck her into bed for a week. He wanted to climb under the covers after her.

She arched her eyebrows. "I get the impression you've just been warned off."

He tipped his chair back on two legs. "By Gowan? Or by you?"

She hesitated. "He's right. There's really no need for you to get involved."

"I am involved. I called him in."

"And now you can let him handle it."

"Is that what you're going to do?"

She blinked at him. "Well, I... I need to take the phone

call. Go to the bank, I guess, in case Bilotti is watching the house. They'll expect me to do that.''

"Fine. I'll drive you.''

"No. I don't want you to get hurt.''

His chair crashed down on all four legs. "Then stop shutting me out, damn it. Stop treating me like some stud you picked up for the night and let me go with you.''

She looked like he'd just stunned her with a two-by-four. "Is that how you feel? Like a stud?''

He stood. "Forget it.''

"Is that some carpenter's term?''

He glared at her.

The amusement in her eyes shimmered into something else, something soft and deep. She stepped up to him, all proud and fine and in his way, and then she took his hands between hers and ducked her head and kissed his fingers. His heart stuttered with surprise.

"I didn't want to make assumptions based on the fact that we—that we slept together. You're not obligated to me. I didn't like to ask.''

"Maybe I need you to ask,'' he said hoarsely. "Maybe I like thinking you feel I'm good for something.''

"What I feel... You've been wonderful. Your support has been wonderful. It's just not what I'm used to.''

She made his head spin. "Yeah, well, you're not what I'm used to, either,'' he muttered.

She dropped his hands. "I'm aware of that.''

"Hey.'' He made a grab for her. "I'm not saying there haven't been other women.''

"Young, pretty ones.''

"Mostly,'' he admitted, enjoying the flash in her eyes. "But mostly those relationships have been one-sided. With you... It's like working with a good piece of wood, being with you. I want to turn it around, see all the sides, get to know the grain and the stress and the flow of it. I have feelings for you. It's okay for you to lean on me some."

She sighed. "I don't know if I can."

Because she didn't know how, he realized. Who in her life—her vague mother, her irresponsible husband, her vulnerable kids—had ever encouraged her to trust them with her burdens? And who was Sean to swear he wouldn't one day let her down?

"Look, you need somebody," he said stubbornly. "Maybe I'm not all you need, but I'm here."

For now, Rachel thought. And maybe she could convince her heart that "for now" was enough.

"The kids will love it out at Patrick's," he continued persuasively. "My nephew Jack is Chris's age. They've got the room and a trampoline. Kittens in the barn."

It sounded like heaven. Lindsey would love the kittens.

"They could go to a motel," she said.

"Too expensive. And they'd be safer at Patrick's. He's a former marine. Hell, my sister-in-law's a doctor."

Compared to her children's safety, what did the danger to her heart matter?

"What would you tell them?"

"How about the truth?"

"No. I can't. Doug…" She made a helpless gesture.

"I don't think you should fret about loyalty to your late husband at this point, Rachel."

She put up her chin. "It's not just that. I don't want to worry the children."

Reluctant respect gleamed in his eyes. "Fine. Then we'll say you're a friend in a jam."

"When would we go?" she asked.

"Dinner, tomorrow? They could pack overnight bags.

Then whatever happens Sunday, you'll know they're taken care of.''

"What about Mama?"

"I told you. She's welcome, too. It'll work." His big hands kneaded her shoulders. "We'll make it work."

She wanted desperately to believe him.

But when she brought up the plan to her mother that evening, Myra's face creased with puzzlement.

"Dinner sounds very pleasant. But why on earth would his brother's family invite us to spend the night?"

"Well…" Rachel swished water around in the sink, grateful to have something to occupy her hands. They were washing up after dinner, while the children chased fireflies across the lawn outside. "Sean felt the children might like to stick around the next day. They have kittens.''

Myra looked even more bewildered. "Kittens?"

Frustration gnawed at Rachel's control. "Forget the kittens," she snapped. "I think it would be good for the children to go."

Safer.

Sean, lounging at the kitchen table with a cup of coffee, spoke up. "It's a longish drive back after dark, Mrs. Jordan. Better for you and the kids to make a weekend out of it."

"But Rachel said you two were coming back here."

He held her gaze. "Exactly."

"Oo-hh." Myra's cheeks pinked with comprehension. Her eyes darted slyly from Sean to Rachel and back again. Rachel wanted to hide her head in the soapy water and never come up for air. "I see. Well, I suppose it would be nice to get away for a little while…"

"You deliberately implied we were coming back to be

alone together," Rachel fumed later, when her mother was safely parked in front of a rerun of *Providence*.

Sean hung a dish towel over the bar on the stove. Another time it would have made her smile, the domesticated gesture from this untamed male. "Do you know any other reason she would have accepted?"

"But now she'll think we want to have sex!"

He grinned at her. "Don't we?"

Rachel fumbled. Heaven help her, she did. She thought about it all the time. Sean's mouth, Sean's hands, Sean's body on hers. Her knees were red from rubbing on the quilted pad. A tiny string of bruises decorated her hip. And every twinge, every chafe, every ache, reminded her how much she wanted him.

It was ridiculous, she thought the next morning as she tugged on her shorts to cover the marks of Sean's fingers. Adolescent. She was a grown woman with two children. She was waiting for a phone call from an extortionist who had threatened to burn her mother's house down around their ears, and all she could think about was how quickly she could leave her family at a stranger's farm so she could get naked with Sean MacNeill.

Rachel cringed. Oh, dear. Oh, no. She was *not* going to be like her mother, so dazzled by some romantic prospect that she would neglect her responsibilities to her own children.

So after breakfast, she was very, very attentive to Chris and Lindsey. She held on to her patience when Chris threw a ball that broke a living room lamp. She clung to her sense of humor when Lindsey sulked at being made to go to the MacNeill farm after practically *promising* Jackie Pittman that they could have a sleep-over that night.

And every time the phone rang, she took deep breaths

and pushed away the thought of Carmine Bilotti on the other end of the line.

Fear and sex were making her insane. Maybe she should make a bargain with God. *You keep my mother and children safe,* she prayed, *and I'll never entertain a wicked thought again.*

And then Chris broke the lamp, and Sean showed up with a tool belt around his hips and a promise in his eyes, and Rachel almost melted with lust.

Remember your bargain, she ordered herself, and treated him with brisk friendliness. Sean gave her a what-the-hell's-going-on look, which she pretended not to see. Eventually he got the hint, because he carried Chris off for a lecture on responsibility and a short course in re-wiring.

Rachel breathed easier. She could manage her libido better when temptation was out of sight. She started slicing tomatoes for sandwiches, feeling almost virtuous.

Lindsey grumbled as she poured two glasses full of milk. "But why do we have to go *this* weekend?"

"Because we were invited for this weekend," Rachel said. And tomorrow she had to deliver a wired drop bag full of phony money to an unknown location or risk her mother's house burning down, but she wasn't telling her daughter that. "Doesn't it sound like fun?"

"I guess." Lindsey carried the full glasses to the table. One slopped over as she set it down. She bit her lip, her head bent as she stared at the spreading white ring.

Rachel grabbed a sponge. "It's okay, sweetie. Pick up the glass."

Lindsey complied. "Is this because we have to meet his family?" she asked diffidently.

"Whose family?" Rachel asked, mopping the spill.

"Sean's. Is he, like, your boyfriend now or something?"

Or something.

Guilt slammed into Rachel. Forget the Scarlet Letter. Her red face gave her away. She took a deep breath. It was bad enough dealing with her mother's suppositions. There was no way she was explaining her relationship with Sean MacNeill to her innocent, fatherless child.

"Well, he's...I think he's very nice," she said carefully. "Don't you?"

Lindsey turned around from the table. "That is so lame, Mom. Are you guys dating?"

"No." Surely that wasn't a lie? Star-shaking, earth-moving sex in the back of a pickup truck was not a date. Rachel studied her daughter's tight face, trying to figure out what Lindsey needed. "Would you mind? Not that I am seeing anyone, but if I were?"

One shoulder raised in a ten-year-old's shrug. "I don't know. Jackie says you two are probably dating. She thinks Sean is hot."

Rachel made a mental note to talk with Deedee Pittman on Monday. "And what did you say?"

"I told her you were too old."

Rachel blinked, not sure if she should be grateful for this reprieve or not. "Oh."

"I didn't mean really old," Lindsey added. "You're still pretty. I just meant you probably weren't interested in boys and stuff. Because you loved Daddy, didn't you?"

Rachel's heart lurched at the anxious note in her daughter's voice. Whatever problems their marriage had, Lindsey had adored her father. "Yes, I did. When we got married, I loved your daddy very much."

Lindsey nodded, a little of the tension leaving her body. "That's what I told Jackie. I mean, it wouldn't be so bad if you were going out with somebody cool like Sean, but I figured you probably weren't interested."

Interested? She was obsessed. Smitten. Besotted.

And it didn't matter, Rachel thought, cold certainty balling in her stomach. It couldn't matter. Her children had lost their father and their home. They were being threatened by criminals, for heaven's sake. They needed to know that their mother, at least, would always be there for them.

Assuming, of course, she survived whatever Bilotti had planned for tomorrow.

"The only thing I'm interested in is getting us all settled down here," she said firmly. "You and me and Chris."

"So, we're not, like, moving again?"

Oh, her poor baby. "Maybe to an apartment. Sometime. You'd like your own bedroom again, right?"

"Yes." Lindsey looked at her sideways, the uncertainty in her eyes tearing at Rachel's heart. "Grandma said we were going to stay there. At the farm."

"Only overnight, sweetie, because I have a lot to do on Sunday." She put her arms protectively around her daughter's sturdy shoulders. The top of Lindsey's head almost reached her chin. So tall, Rachel thought, and yet the skin at the back of her neck was still baby fine. "Does that sound okay?"

Lindsey nodded against her rib cage, and Rachel's chest squeezed with fierce maternal love.

"Nothing has changed," she vowed. "Nothing is going to change. Mr. MacNeill is a friend, that's all."

The screen door swung open and he was there, silhouetted by sunshine, all knowing dark eyes and untamed black hair, holding the repaired lamp.

He raised one eyebrow, not saying anything. So, he'd

heard. Regret stopped her breath. Should she apologize? Explain? But before she could speak, the phone shrilled on the wall. She jumped.

"I'll get it," Lindsey offered.

"No!" Rachel blurted.

"Got it," Sean said at the same time.

Crossing the kitchen in long, quick strides, he lifted the receiver. Another kind of tension built in Rachel. He listened a moment and then, following Gowan's instructions, handed her the phone.

"Is it...?"

His eyes narrowed with warning. His mouth was grim. "It's for you," he said.

Chapter 12

Her palms were sweaty on the steering wheel.

Relax, Rachel ordered herself. An overnight at a farm in Jefferson County was hardly exile in an alien land. Chris was raring to go. Even Lindsey had warmed to the trip after Sean invited the children to ride with him in his truck. Rachel could see her daughter's dark ponytail through the rear window ahead. And anything was preferable to leaving them at home, a target for the Bilottis.

Ten o'clock tomorrow morning, Carmine had demanded on the phone. *All the nice folks will be at church or in bed. You bring the money in a brown grocery bag to the parking lot behind the high school. You come alone, and you don't tell anybody where you're going. Or you better be sure your mother's all paid up on her fire insurance.*

Rachel shivered and gripped the wheel tighter. The road dipped up and down and under the branches of an ancient oak.

"Oh, how pretty," Myra said, leaning forward to peer through the windshield.

Rachel looked past a tangle of pink shrub roses. White between green lawn and dark pines, a two-story farmhouse gleamed in the afternoon sun. An old building with new paint, a gray barn and a weathered fence, it looked rooted in the Carolina clay in a way Rachel hadn't expected from a house belonging to the pilot brother of a Yankee carpenter. It looked well-kept. Welcoming. Solid. Wistfulness clutched her. It looked exactly like the kind of house she'd wanted to live in as a child. There was even a basketball hoop mounted over the barn door.

She had no business dragging her mother and her children and her problems to this place, like a cat depositing dead mice on the doorstep, messy and unwelcome.

"Very pretty," she said.

The red truck rumbled down the long drive and stopped by the walk. Rachel pulled in behind. Sean swung out of the cab, all long legs and easy grace. The passenger door opened more slowly, and Lindsey hopped down.

"Uncle Sean!"

As Rachel got out of her car, a boy bolted from the house, a big golden dog running at his heels.

Sean grinned. "Hey, buddy."

The child launched himself from two yards away. Rachel watched Sean catch and whirl him around before dumping him on his feet. Close up, she could see the boy had his uncle's dark hair and grin. She could see, too, that the left side of his face was red and puckered with scars.

Beside her, Myra caught her breath in shock. Please God, don't let her say something tactless, Rachel prayed. She opened her mouth.

But Lindsey had already planted herself in front of them. "Sean says you have kittens in your barn."

Half a head shorter, the boy smiled up at her with all his uncle's charm. "Yeah. Want to see?"

"Okay."

"I want to see," Chris said.

Sean cocked an eyebrow in Rachel's direction. "Is that all right with you?"

"I... Of course," she said, feeling more than ever that things were moving out of her hands.

"Have fun," Sean said to his nephew. "Where's your mom?"

"She's coming. Um..." Collecting his manners, the boy smiled at Rachel. "Nice to meet you."

She was captivated, and gave him her best First Day of School smile in response. "Nice to meet you, too."

The boy's voice carried back to them as the three children walked to the barn. "Dad says the kittens are, like, four weeks old. Their eyes are open and everything, but we have to be careful not to let them out yet."

"That poor boy," Myra breathed. "What happened to his face?"

Sean's expression tightened. "Jack? He was in a car accident when he was a baby. I told the kids about it on the ride over. But he's fine now."

Rachel was impressed, both by Sean's dismissal of his nephew's scars and his sensitivity in preparing her children to meet him.

"Lindsey liked him," she offered, which was a pretty lame thing to say, but it was enough to earn her one of Sean's warm looks.

"I thought I heard the truck."

A short, tidy woman with shrewd brown eyes and masses of light brown hair stepped from the porch. She kissed her brother-in-law on the cheek and then smiled at Myra and Rachel.

"Kate MacNeill." She introduced herself. "I'm so glad you could come."

Rachel wondered what her hostess would say if she knew the whole story behind this visit. But Sean had told his brother as little as possible, honoring Rachel's insistence that they pretend everything was normal. She hadn't considered how awkward her omission would make her feel. "I'm sorry to impose on you on such short notice."

"Not at all. We're used to company." Kate's gaze was frank, assessing. "Though Sean doesn't bring friends by very often."

Friends? Did she mean, *women?*

"Don't overthink it, beautiful," Sean said, taking Rachel's elbow and steering her toward the house. "I want Patrick to meet her," he told his sister-in-law. "Is he inside?"

"In the kitchen. Val has him chopping vegetables or something. I'm a terrible hostess," Kate confided to the other two women. "I make my guests cook."

Sean grinned wickedly. "And we like it that way. Kate's a doctor. We're afraid if we make her cook, she'll put syringes in the soup."

"I'll give you syringes," she warned him.

Lowering his head, he kissed her with obvious affection. "Can I pick where?"

Behind them, the screen door opened. "You want to stop flirting with my wife long enough to introduce me to our guests?" a deep voice inquired.

This had to be Patrick. Rachel studied him as he shook her mother's hand. Shorter and broader than his youngest brother, with close-cropped dark hair and piercing blue eyes, Patrick MacNeill radiated quiet strength. He looked, she thought, a lot like Sean would look in another eight or ten years.

Myra sighed with pleasure at being in the presence of two such beautiful men. Rachel felt a little breathless herself.

"Nice to meet you," Patrick said noncommittally. His big palm engulfed hers.

Rachel fought the sense of being judged and found wanting. "I appreciate you having us."

"Couldn't say no to Sean."

"Very few people can say no to my brother-in-law." A very pretty, very pregnant blonde with a trio of silver hoops in one ear came out on the porch. She directed a friendly smile at Rachel. "Hi. I'm Val."

"Very few *women* can say no." The screen door swung again, and another big, outrageously handsome man joined them on the porch. Rachel looked up into amused blue eyes set in a lean, clever face.

Sean hadn't told him anything, she decided.

"Con MacNeill," the giant said.

"Rachel Fuller."

Once more, her hand was enclosed in a massive grip. "It's a pleasure."

"Dibs," Sean said briefly.

Everyone on the porch goggled at him. Con released her hand slowly.

"Excuse me," Rachel said. "Did you say, 'dibs'?"

"Yeah. It means, like, 'I call' or—"

She was hot with embarrassment. And more thrilled than she wanted to admit, even to herself, by his possessiveness. "I know what it means. I can't believe you said it."

"Sean will say anything." The pretty blonde smiled again.

"We've just had more practice ignoring him," Con added.

Rachel felt like Alice down the rabbit hole. She looked to the nearest likely adult for rescue. "Are they always this bad?"

Kate MacNeill laughed. "No. Sometimes they're worse. You get used to it."

Would she? Would she have the chance?

She watched, fascinated and a little resistant, as the MacNeill clan opened and encompassed them, sweeping her own family away on a tide of warmth. Myra was carried off to the kitchen to drink iced tea and help Val make potato salad. The children, straggling back from the barn, were co-opted into an impromptu baseball game, siding with Sean against his brothers and Jack.

And Rachel was left stranded on the front porch with sharp-eyed Kate MacNeill.

The other woman sank into a rocker with a sigh. A curly haired girl toddled from the house and demanded to be held on her lap. Kate complied, confiding, "It feels good to sit. I was on call last night. Didn't get home till three."

Rachel shifted on her own chair—one of Sean's, she noted absently, stroking her hand over the arm as if she could draw strength from the wood. "I hope we're not putting you out too much."

"Oh, no. Sean explained you had some kind of emergency?" When Rachel didn't elaborate, Kate shrugged and continued. "Besides, we were all eager to see the woman who had our Sean so excited."

Rachel was flattered. Touched. Embarrassed. It was bad enough that she wasn't being completely open about the kind of emergency that forced her to rely on the compassion of strangers. She didn't want to give them the wrong idea about her relationship with Sean as well.

"He's just being kind," she said.

"He is kind," Kate agreed. "But he wouldn't have invited you here out of kindness."

Rachel looked over the lawn, where Con, as catcher, and Sean, as batter, were going head-to-head over a strike call. Chris was following the argument from first base, eyes wide, grin nearly splitting his face. Guy stuff. Despite her own discomfort, she felt her lips curve upward in a smile.

"And he's good with children," Kate said.

"He is." Rachel could see that. She could picture him with babies of his own, a girl with his impudent dark eyes, a boy with his jaunty grin. Yearning almost stole her breath. And then she sighed. Sean MacNeill didn't want to be anybody's daddy. No matter how effective he was against bullies, she wouldn't saddle him with her children or her problems.

"But I can't expect him to take responsibility for mine," she said. "It's different when they're your own."

"Mmm." Kate nuzzled her little girl's neck, making her giggle with delight. "That's what Patrick thought before he met me."

"You're not—"

"I'm Jack's stepmother."

Rachel frowned ruefully. "I've just been rude, haven't I?"

"Not rude. Maybe a little set in your thinking? Children take love where they find it. And goodness knows, Sean has a lot of love to give."

"Yes," Rachel said dryly. "And he spreads it around, too."

Kate laughed. "Go ahead and tell me to mind my own business. I admit I'm fond of my brother-in-law. I guess I don't want to see him hurt by the same mistake twice."

"What mistake?"

"Hey, beautiful!" Sean loped to the porch, sun on his hair and in his eyes, exuding heat and pheromones. She was dazzled by him, her brain flooded with sunshine, her chest with warmth.

"We're getting clobbered here," he said, squinting up at her. "I'm recruiting you for our team."

Con hefted the bat over his shoulder. "As what?"

"Relief pitcher."

His brother snorted. "In a family game? Get real."

"Aw, let her play, Uncle Con," Jack said, adding unwisely, "She's just a girl."

Patrick grinned. "Uh-oh."

"Fighting words," murmured Kate. "*Can* you pitch?"

Rachel was tired of inaction, of sitting on the sidelines. Here, at last, was an arena she could fight in. "I can pitch."

"Then get 'em, girl."

She belonged, Sean thought with satisfaction as they all trooped back to the house to clean up for dinner, laughing and sweaty and dirty, crowing over runs scored and talking big about "next time." His relief pitcher had struck out the mighty Con and given Jack a piece of the ball that landed him a double. And they'd won. Rachel glowed with victory. Her lovely long legs were stained with grass and dirt from sliding into third, and her face was pink with exertion.

He wanted to back her up against the side of the house and plunge into her like a diver into water.

Later, he promised himself.

For now it was enough to have her here, laughing with Kate, complimenting some new recipe Val was trying out for her restaurant. Always appreciative of women, all women, he took a moment to enjoy the contrasts between them: Kate, calm and tidy in her catalog clothes, and Val, like a pregnant fairy queen in her flowing skirts and jewelry, and Rachel, in shorts and dirt, towering over them both.

But she fit in, he thought with pride. Her family fit in. Her mother was soaking up Con's attention as they stringed beans into a colander. Chris and Jack had their heads together, sneaking sodas from the fridge when they thought no one was looking. The comfortable chaos reminded Sean pleasantly of childhood dinners, of Thanksgivings with his uncles watching football and his aunts in the kitchen and his cousins—Ross and Luke and Maggie and Mick—crowded around the table of his parents' house in Quincy.

It felt good. Right.

None of which stopped his slow burn when he looked over and saw Rachel talking earnestly with Patrick about some school bond issue. Sean had told her straight-up and early on he didn't care beans about the five years' difference between them, but there was no getting around the fact that Patrick was nearer her age than he was. More nearly her equal in education, too, Sean thought bleakly. Hell, either of his brothers was more her type: steady, settled and financially secure.

He was a chump to be thinking Thanksgiving dinner when all she wanted from him was sex in the back of his truck.

Nothing is going to change. Mr. MacNeill is a friend, that's all.

Sean scowled.

"Why the long face, bro?"

Pride demanded he deny it. "I'm thinking."

Con's amused gaze flicked to Rachel and back. "I can see how that would be a strain," he drawled, and then winced as his wife kicked him under the table. He changed the subject. "I brought your business plan for the loan application along. We can go over it after dinner."

"Yeah?" Despite his cool pose, Sean felt his heart begin to hammer. "Think the bank will go for it?"

Con shrugged. "Who can say? Looks good, though. Well thought out."

Sean hid his flash of pleasure at his brother's praise. "Did you include those photos I sent?"

"Of the wardrobe and chairs and things? Yeah. They should help. You sure you want to put the truck up as collateral, though?"

Sean squelched his brief regret. He wasn't going to fail. "Don't have any choice."

Patrick spoke up. "You know, Con and I talked it over. We'd be willing to—"

"No." And if he did fail, it would be on his own. "I appreciate the help with the proposal, though."

"We just want to see you protect your cash flow."

Con nodded. "A lot of start-up businesses fold because they're under-capitalized."

"Mine almost did," Val added.

Sean couldn't resent his family's interference. Not when it was so clearly motivated by concern. But he wished they wouldn't emphasize what a gamble he was taking with Rachel sitting right there, listening to every word.

"That's why I'm applying for the loan," he said evenly.

"And his business is not going to fold," Rachel declared in her schoolteacher tone. "His furniture is beautiful. He can sell as much as he makes, and he works extremely hard. Of course he'll do well."

Con raised his eyebrows. "She sounds like Mom."

"Well." Patrick cleared his throat. "Looks like we'd better take this new...venture seriously, then."

"Very seriously," Val said with a twinkle.

They weren't talking about the furniture business anymore. Sean wondered if Rachel caught on. Her brow creased uncertainly as she looked around the circle of amused and interested faces.

But later, as Sean carried plates to the dining room, Patrick stopped him with a hand on his arm.

"I don't know what you're getting into here," his brother said. "Do you?"

Sean scowled. "I'm not looking to hurt her, if that's what you mean."

"No. I'm more concerned with whether she could hurt you. This mess that she's in—are you sure it's your fight?"

The same thought had bothered Sean. He shook it away. Rachel and her kids *needed* him. "Since when did you start worrying about me getting into fights?"

"Maybe now that you're grown up, I don't want to see anything happen to that pretty face of yours."

Sean ran his hand over his face. He was the only MacNeill brother to survive adolescence with an unbroken nose. He shrugged. "So, if I'm grown up now, maybe I've got more important things to worry about."

He went through to the dining room, where Rachel was setting forks around the table.

She looked up, her pretty mouth compressed with concern. "I hope I didn't offend your family earlier, speaking out like that."

Offend them? Con, at least, was delighted to watch him take the fall at last. "You didn't offend them."

"I didn't mean to embarrass you."

"You didn't embarrass me."

She set her plates down on the table. "It just made me see red when you're so clearly qualified and committed to doing this, and they did their big-brother-knows-best routine."

"Rachel." He was shaken by her faith in him. He backed her into the china cabinet and caught her chin between his thumb and forefinger, enjoying the way her mahogany eyes went wide. "I don't need your support against my brothers. But I like having you in my corner. I like it a lot."

He bent his head and laid his lips on hers. The kiss started smooth and soft and easy. A gesture of thanks. And then the hitch in her breath hooked him and her warm scent reeled him in, and he wanted—needed—more. He kissed her again, urged her lips to part and her tongue to play with his.

And cool-schoolteacher Rachel, let's-be-friends Rachel, nothing's-going-to-change Rachel, put her arms around him and kissed him back.

He took it deeper, savoring her quick shudder against him. Friends, my butt, he thought with delight.

Her hands tightened in his hair and he stopped thinking at all. There was only Rachel, her smooth warm skin and her hot slick mouth and the hunger in her that woke a primitive need in him. He leaned into her, pushed against her with enough force to make the glasses inside the old pine breakfront chime together. The sound sang in his ears, recalled him to their surroundings.

He couldn't take her in his brother's dining room with their families about to walk in any minute.

Sean lifted his head.

And saw Rachel's ten-year-old daughter watching them through the doorway to the living room.

"Hell," he said.

Lindsey turned and ran.

"What?" Rachel's mouth was red from his kisses. Her eyes were wide and worried. "What is it?"

"Nothing," he muttered. "I hope it's nothing. I'll be right back."

Sean found Lindsey in the barn, curled in the kittens' stall. She spared him one long, cool look when he showed up and then stared stubbornly down at the straw by her feet.

That was all right, Sean told himself, trying to ignore the sympathetic lurch of his heart at the miserable set of her mouth. He'd had females mad at him before.

He knew better than to ask if he could come in. He unlatched the stall, making the four black-and-white kittens inside scatter, and closed it behind him.

"You want to talk?" he asked.

"No."

"Fine. I'll talk. You can listen." He looked around for a seat. Found it on the bin that held the pet food. It creaked under his weight. "You saw me with your mom."

Her chin angled up. "You were kissing her."

So much for not talking. "Yeah, I was."

"She said you were 'friends.'" Scorn and betrayal vibrated in Lindsey's voice.

"Yeah, I heard her." He studied her averted face. He wished he had Patrick's experience at fathering. He envied Con his smooth way of reasoning. All Seán had to go on was his knowledge of the female species and his affection for this one particular child. He hoped they would be enough. "So, are you mad because you think she lied to you, or mad because I kissed her?"

Lindsey lifted one shoulder. "She never tells me what's going on."

Sean sympathized with her frustration. "That's her way of trying to protect you."

She looked at him directly for the first time. "Will you tell me?"

"I can't tell you everything," Sean said cautiously. He'd come out here to make things right for Rachel. But meeting Lindsey's suspiciously shiny eyes, he realized he wanted to do right by her daughter as well. And that didn't include more lies. "If you ask me stuff I can answer, I will."

Lindsey looked back at the kittens. One of them, a black-and-white puffball, was batting a leaf across the hard-packed floor. "Are you her boyfriend?"

"I've got feelings for your mom," Sean said quietly. "And I'm hoping she's got feelings for me. I don't know if we've figured out what to do about all those feelings yet."

"But you're grown-ups."

Right. "And she's your mom. She loves you. She loves you and Chris more than anything. She's got to look at what it would mean to you before she gets mixed up with me."

The child's gaze slid sideways again. "You're all right," she muttered.

Warmth bloomed in his chest. He felt like she'd given him season tickets to the Celtics. Center court.

"I like you, too," he said.

"But I'm still mad at my mom."

Well. Sean shifted on the pet food bin. "Sometimes," he said slowly, "it's easier to be mad at the parent who stays than the parent who goes away. My dad, he was a marine."

Lindsey watched the black-and-white kitten corner the leaf and pounce. But he could tell she was listening. It was there, in the angle of her head, in the tension in her neck. "So?"

"So, he was gone a lot when I was growing up. Overseas. I missed him, but I didn't talk about it much. I was afraid it would make my mom sad. And I didn't want my brothers to think I was a baby."

"I miss my daddy," Lindsey said to the kitten.

"I know you do, honey." Anger filled him at the man who had been her father, who had skipped out on his responsibilities and her love. But anger wouldn't help Lindsey. "It used to make me mad, too," Sean said. "When my dad went away. Like he didn't love us enough to stay and take care of us. I couldn't take it out on him, because he wasn't around. And maybe I worried he didn't want to be around."

Lindsey bent her head. There was a tiny pleat between her brows, a pout to her lower lip. She looked so much like Rachel that Sean's heart turned over in his chest.

"Sometimes I was a real jerk about it," he continued. "Really gave my mom a hard time, until my brother pounded on me some. Patrick," he explained, when her head came up in surprise. "I had to be a little older before I accepted that being away was part of our dad's job. That *was* how he took care of us."

"My daddy killed himself," Lindsey whispered.

"Yeah. I know. Only the way I figure it, maybe he was still taking care of you the best way he knew how, because he owed so many people money."

Her face set. "I don't care about the money. He shouldn't have gone away."

He stroked her hair. "I know."

And before he had time to prepare, before he could shield his emotions, she ambushed him. His arms were full of little girl, bony knees and silky hair and streaming eyes. She cried as though she had a right to soak his shirt and break his heart.

He was in for it now, Sean thought. He didn't want to do this, didn't want to fall for a kid he couldn't claim and couldn't protect. Panic almost made him bolt the barn. But he stuck, because this kid didn't have anywhere to run and no one else to turn to. He held her until her tears melted his last resistance and she was quiet in his arms, nestled in a corner of his heart that had been empty for twelve restless years.

"Better?" he asked.

She sniffed and wiped her nose with the back of her hand.

He lifted enough to dig his handkerchief out of his back pocket. "Here."

She regarded it doubtfully. "Mom has tissues."

"That's because she's a mom. Goes with the territory. My mother taught me to carry a handkerchief." When she still made no move to take it, he dried the tears from her flushed smooth cheeks himself.

"But you've got to blow your own nose," he said, trying for stern, and got a watery chuckle in response.

She blew her nose, hard, and then offered the handkerchief back.

"Stick it in your pocket," he suggested.

"I'm sorry," she said.

"'S'all right."

She sighed and relaxed against him. With the wailing done, the puffball kitten wobbled over to investigate. Lindsey almost—*almost*—smiled. And inspiration hit Sean over the head like a two-by-four.

"Patrick's not going to want all these cats around in a couple of weeks," he said. "I was thinking I might take one off his hands."

"You want a kitten?" Hope quavered in her voice.

He'd never had responsibility for an animal in his life. He traveled too much, job site to job site. A pet required things, like being home at night and regular trips to the grocery store.

"Yeah," he said firmly. "I do. You want to help me pick one out?"

She leaned from his lap to stroke the black-and-white kitten with one finger. "Jack said they couldn't leave their mother yet."

"They're too young now," Sean agreed. "But later, most of them will need another home. That's the way things are with cats."

Very daring now, Fuzzball made a try for the girl's lap. Sean winced as kitty claws pricked through his jeans. Lindsey unhooked the animal from his knee and buried her nose in soft kitten fur.

"It would miss its mom," she said, the words muffled. *I miss my daddy.*

Sean nodded gravely. "Nobody could take the place of its real parent. But that doesn't mean somebody else, somebody lucky enough to take it home, couldn't love it. Maybe you could come by sometimes to visit. Give it attention. Do stuff with it, maybe—and then it wouldn't miss its real mom so much."

She looked up at him, her nose still red from crying and her eyes vulnerable. "Do you think so?"

There was an odd pressure in his chest. "Yeah, I think so. It might be tough at first, but I bet after a while it would be okay."

She set the kitten down. It wandered around, its tail a fuzzy question mark, until one of its siblings jumped it. Lindsey laughed. After a while her hand crept into Sean's.

"I think so, too," she said.

Deep satisfaction filled him. Deep uneasiness. He was committed now to more than a kitten.

They were still sitting hand in hand, watching the kittens play, when Rachel came to call them into dinner.

Chapter 13

The porch light was on. Her mother's house was dark and quiet, white curtains unmoving behind unbroken windows. No flames shot from the roof, no sirens disturbed the night. Rachel got out of the car with a sense of relief so sharp it felt like disappointment.

Sean's truck door slammed. He sauntered toward her with that gorgeous male walk of his, confident and aware inside his long-boned body.

Desire dried her mouth. Not now, Rachel thought. She shouldn't be having these lustful, inappropriate thoughts now. Maybe when all this was over… No. Not then, either. The realization sunk in her stomach like a stone. Never again. She had her children to worry about, and her mother, and while Myra might have no judgment at all, Rachel wasn't going to do anything to compromise the safe and stable life her babies needed.

"You didn't need to come back with me," she said.

"I'm sure your brother would have liked you to spend the night."

"My brother would kick my butt if he knew the kind of danger you were in and I didn't come back with you. You shouldn't be alone in the house. You're not safe."

"And I'm so much safer with you sleeping in the garage?"

He sent her a long, level look, and her heart gave a quick, undisciplined thump. "I'm not sleeping in the garage tonight."

Heavens. Her face, her whole body, flushed and throbbed. She started down the walk with short, quick steps. Remember the children, she instructed herself.

"What were you and Lindsey talking about before dinner?" she asked when they reached the porch.

He held out his hand for her keys. "Oh, I told her we could get a kitten."

"A kitten?" Rachel didn't know whether she was amused or appalled.

"Is that a problem? You don't like cats," he guessed.

"I love cats," she said automatically. "Doug was the one who... Anyway, my mother doesn't want a pet. You should have discussed this with me first."

He plucked the keys from her grasp. "Didn't have to. It's my cat. Mine and Lindsey's. It'll stay with me, in the garage."

She could live with him taking her keys. But a pet for her children... He had no right to decide on something so important.

Irritated, she said, "That's an awfully big commitment."

"I can afford cat food, Rachel."

"Not of money. Of your time."

He unlocked the front door. "I don't mind. Lindsey needs a pet."

"Lindsey needs a lot of things since her father died. She shouldn't expect you to provide them."

"Why not, if I'm willing?"

"Because you won't always be around."

"That's your assumption."

"I don't want to see her get hurt."

He switched on a lamp and regarded her steadily in the yellow glow. "Are we still talking about Lindsey here?"

She started to shake. He understood women too well. He saw her too clearly. Had he known she was falling in love with him before she realized it herself?

"I don't want to see her hurt," she repeated stubbornly. "After my father died, there were too many men who came and went in my mother's life. In my life. I don't want that for my daughter."

He tensed. "Any creeps?"

She loved him for his immediate protective response. "Was I abused, do you mean?" She shook her head. "No. Once, when I was fifteen...but Mama sent him packing."

He brushed his knuckle against her cheek. "I'm sorry."

The tender gesture brought tears to her eyes. She blinked them away. "It was all right. I was all right. In a way, the nice guys were worse. You give away enough little pieces of your heart, you don't have much left. You start to wonder what makes the good ones all go away. Is there something the matter with your mother? Or is it your fault that none of them ever stay?"

"Maybe they wanted to stay. Maybe they didn't have a choice."

"Or maybe they just didn't care."

"Bull. I cared."

Cared. Past tense. Rachel frowned. "What are you talking about?"

"Look, I'm not saying I'm Mr. Commitment. I've walked away from plenty of relationships. But the only time I ever walked out on a little girl it was because her mother took her away."

Her heart stopped. "You have a little girl?"

He raked his hair with his fingers. "I thought I did. For three months, twelve years ago."

She closed her eyes to do the math. "The high school girlfriend."

"Bingo."

"She got pregnant?"

"Right after we broke up. Only she shows up five months into it and tells me the baby's mine."

"What did you do?"

"What could I do? I quit school. Trina didn't want to get married. I pushed for it, but she said no."

"But you supported her." Rachel was sure of it.

"Hell, yes. I had to. Her parents kicked her out when they found out about the baby. We got a little apartment in Dorchester, and I got a job working construction with my cousin Ross."

She thought of his strong, cohesive family, his solidly successful brothers. "That must have been hard," she said softly.

He shrugged. "It was no picnic. I had to be gone all day, and Trina cried all the time. Well, if we'd gotten along, we wouldn't have split up in the first place. But then Alyson was born, and it all seemed worthwhile."

"Alyson?" she prompted.

"My—Trina's daughter."

"You loved her."

"From the moment she was born. Trina had a rough

time in delivery, so I took over getting up with the baby at night. She was so small." His voice was full of remembered wonder. "Small and perfect. She wasn't fussy. I'd go to pick her up and she'd look at me like I hung the moon, you know?"

Rachel knew. "What happened?"

"I came home from work one night—Alyson was three months old—and Trina tells me, all excited, that her baby's 'real father' has had a change of heart. Like all of a sudden, he wants them, so I'm supposed to disappear."

"What did you do?"

"Nothing," he said bleakly. "There wasn't a damn thing I could do. My name wasn't even on the birth certificate. Guess she was afraid she'd lose her meal ticket if she named the other guy, and she loved him enough not to name me. So instead of a father, Alyson had this big blank."

Rachel admired his willingness to shoulder his teenage responsibilities. Ached for his loss. And understood so much more about his reluctance to give his heart away.

"You were her father in every way that mattered."

Sean wanted to believe her. But even he wasn't that big a chump. "Right. The kid will never remember me."

"It's a child's first relationships that form the basis for the rest of her human attachments," she lectured in her best schoolteacher's voice. "It doesn't matter if she never knows your name. If you loved her, if you held her and talked to her and comforted her when she cried, you've given her a gift that will last the rest of her life."

She was bright-eyed and earnest. Wonderful. Wrong. He hated to bust her bubble, but she had to know how things were. How *he* was.

"I was just day labor, beautiful. That doesn't cut it, in

construction or raising kids. In the long run, I wasn't there for her.''

"Not in the long run," she acknowledged. "But sometimes being there at that moment is the best you can do. Sometimes it's enough."

"Yeah?" He hitched his thumbs in his belt loops. "Was it enough for you?"

Her pretty mouth hung open. He wanted to kiss her. "I…"

He smiled wryly. "I didn't think so."

She flushed. "Uncle Jed," she said suddenly.

"What?"

"Uncle Jed. He hung around the summer after Daddy died. I didn't want to like him. I wasn't liking anybody much that year. But when he and Mama were sitting on the porch, he used to get up and throw a softball with me. I only went along because I figured if he was busy with me he couldn't make eyes at Mama. But I made the softball team my freshman year because of Uncle Jed." Rachel smiled at him then, with her lips and her eyes, and her warmth stole his breath.

"Thank you," she said simply. "I'd forgotten that. So you see—" she caught his big hand, and cradled it in her slim, fine ones, and kissed his scarred knuckle "—temporary relationships can have their own advantages."

He couldn't concentrate with her mouth warm against his fingers. He turned his hand, cupping her jaw. "You think?" he asked hoarsely.

She smiled against his thumb. "I'm almost sure of it."

He rubbed the pad of his thumb across her soft bottom lip. Her eyes were wide. Her lip was slick. Her breath hitched. He leaned in slowly, enjoying the signs of her arousal, following the path of his thumb with his tongue before dipping inside. She was so damn fine: earnest, stubborn, loyal, real. All day long, watching her with her kids, his family, he'd admired and wanted her. He wanted her again. He wanted her now.

He wanted her for always.

He pushed the thought away as her hands, soft and urgent, slid up his back and closed on his shoulders. He didn't want to think. They were alone, and she was willing. They'd wasted enough time dissecting the past. Analyzing his feelings, for crying out loud. And tomorrow... No, he definitely didn't want to think about what she faced tomorrow.

He kissed her again, deeper, longer. Beguiled by each part of her, he kissed the curve of her jaw and the fragrant hollow below her ear and the slope of her breast through her sensible cotton shirt.

She gasped and wriggled against him. "I just want you to know that I'll understand when it's time for you to move on."

He pulled at the hem of her shirt. She was talking crazy talk. "I'm not going anywhere."

Beneath her cotton bra, her dark nipples were plainly visible. Expertly, he dispensed with hooks and slid the bra straps down her shoulders.

The doorbell rang. Rachel stiffened.

Sean swore. "Don't answer it."

She looked at him like he'd lost his mind. "What if it's—?"

"Bilotti? You think he's going to ring the doorbell before he torches the place?"

But she was already fumbling with the straps of her bra, grabbing for her shirt. Frustrated, Sean tucked his hands into his jeans' pockets and stood back while she opened the door.

Gowan. It figured.

The blond agent stood at attention in the circle of yellow porch light, a wide flat box in one hand.

"Anyone order a pizza?"

"Agent Gowan!" Rachel's hands went to her waist as if to make sure she was all tucked in. "Won't you come in?"

His poster-boy smile flickered. Phony. "Lee. Thanks. I tried calling earlier, but no one was home. So I thought I'd come over, make sure you were all right."

"Thank you, I—"

"We're fine," Sean said.

Gowan acknowledged him with a curt nod. "Mac-Neill." He turned back to Rachel. "Kids get off okay?"

"Yes. They're staying with my mother at Sean's brother's." Like a good hostess, she stepped back to admit him farther into the house. "Can I get you something? Coffee? Did you really bring a pizza?"

He lifted the box in his hands. "This? No. This is just a blind, in case Bilotti's watching the house. I wouldn't say no to coffee, though."

"Of course. Sean?"

At least she hadn't told him to get lost. "I'll have a cup. Thanks."

With quick, firm steps, she headed for the kitchen, leaving the two men facing off in the living room like gunslingers in a disputed town.

"What exactly are you doing here, MacNeill?"

Sean bared his teeth in a smile that didn't fool either of them. "Moral support."

"You know she's vulnerable right now."

"That's why I'm here." To protect her, he meant, but he didn't say so. He wasn't explaining himself or his motives to this stuffed shirt.

Rachel came back with a steaming mug in each hand.

She was too pale, Sean thought angrily, and the skin under her eyes looked bruised. "Coffee?"

"Thanks." Gowan took it and set it down, untasted, on Myra's walnut-veneer coffee table. "I have something for you, too."

He shifted a pile of ladies' magazines to accommodate the pizza box and then lifted the top.

Rachel covered her mouth with her hand. "Oh, my goodness."

"That's a lot of money," Sean said.

The agent took out a folded brown Food Lion bag and snapped it open. The pop made her jump. He started to load the bills inside.

"It's all fake. Sixty-four thousand, you said?"

Rachel nodded. It looked real to her. Except that she'd never seen so much money in her life, not even in a Monopoly set. Fake. Funny money. Like in the movies, when the bad guys blew open the bank vault or handed over a suitcase of drug money. She shivered. Only for her, the amount was smaller and the danger was real.

Gowan held up a stack of twenties, indistinguishable from all the others, before placing it in the bag. "This is your transmitter. It will signal your location, but it can't give us your voice. Your radio will be over the driver's side. Turn it on when you start the car."

"How?" Rachel asked.

He palmed a small device, square and black, like a cheap calculator. "Press this round button. It will look like you're adjusting the sun visor. Speak in a normal voice, and we'll hear you."

"When do you make the arrest?" Sean wanted to know.

"We'll have three agents at the high school. Eight on the surrounding roads. If Bilotti is there, we'll get him. If he isn't—say, he's watching from a distance, or he's paid some kid to make the pickup—then we'll wait till he shows. Or we'll follow his delivery boy."

"What about Rachel?"

"We'll be in radio contact." The agent spoke directly to her. "You'll look like you're on your own. You'll feel like you're on your own, but you won't be. It's safer if nobody follows you." He narrowed his eyes at Sean. "Nobody," he emphasized.

Screw you, buddy, Sean thought.

Gowan stood, stuffing his hands into his pockets. "Will you be all right tonight?" he asked Rachel.

She smiled at him and lied. The girl had guts. "I'm fine."

But after Gowan had drunk his coffee and planted his bug and left, Sean said, "I don't like you going alone."

Rachel picked up both coffee cups. "You heard Lee Gowan. They'll be in radio contact."

"It's still a risk."

"It's one I'm willing to take. You were right. I couldn't go on paying forever."

He paced the living room, unable to hold still. "Yeah, well, all of a sudden I get why you did it. I'd pay Bilotti myself, if it would keep that son of a bitch away from you."

She walked into the kitchen. "What did you tell me? I was so afraid of losing, I couldn't win? This way is better."

He followed her. "I don't like thinking I'm responsible for putting you in danger."

She rinsed the cups in the sink. Her sensible summer top revealed her strong shoulders and silky skin. With her head bent, he could see the vulnerable nape of her neck.

"You're not responsible," she said. "I am. But for what it's worth, I have faith in your judgment."

He wasn't sure he did. Not when the stakes were so high. "I don't want to let you down."

She dried her hands on a towel and turned. She was still too pale, but her eyes, on a level with his chin, were warm and direct. "I'll take the chance. Just don't you die on me."

He didn't get it. He was too busy trying to figure if it made him some kind of bastard if he took her to bed now. He was already imagining how she would feel and taste on his tongue. Her words made no sense. She was the one being threatened.

"I won't," he promised, and moved in close.

Her lips were moist and ready. Her hands were damp and soft. His control slipped as he kissed her, as he pushed her back against the sink and felt her thighs part to take him. It was the back of his truck all over again.

He tugged her shirt clear of her waistband and found her sweetness with his mouth. She sighed and cradled his head, holding him to her breast. Need clawed him. He yanked her closer, bending, kneeling, pulling at clothes, seeking more skin, more sweetness, more Rachel. He popped the button of her shorts, jerked on her zipper and...froze.

Strung across the creamy curve of her hip like a faint blue tattoo was a line of tiny bruises.

"Did I do this?" Even to his own ears, his voice sounded harsh.

Above him, Rachel opened her eyes. "Do what?"

"The bruises. Did I mark you?"

"I...don't remember."

Right. He spanned her hip with one hand, until every finger matched and covered a small dark circle. He swore.

She touched his hair. "It doesn't matter."

It mattered to him. She mattered to him, and he'd taken her with all the care of a bulldozer let loose on a stand of prime wood, once in the back of his truck and once— almost—standing up in her mother's kitchen. Way to go, lover boy, he thought derisively.

He lifted his hand and, with his lips, soothed each tiny bruise.

She shivered. "What are you doing?"

"I'm trying to kiss it and make it better," he explained solemnly.

Her laugh was shaky. Raw sex didn't embarrass her, he thought with a twist of heart. But a little consideration left her pink-cheeked and uncertain.

She tried to cover the marks with her hand. "I don't think that works."

"Then we'll have to find something that does," he said, and stood and lifted her in his arms.

"Put me down," she said as he carried her through the living room.

He started up the stairs. "In a minute."

"I'm too heavy."

She wasn't light. "I can't," he said. "It's a macho thing. I don't make it to the bed with you, I won't feel manly."

Would she buy that? Her smile bloomed. God, he loved her smile. "Then by all means, let's make it to the bed."

He pushed open the door to her room. The blue-flowered wallpaper and limp white curtains hadn't changed since he'd slept there alone. The room still smelled like flowers. Rachel's worn running shoes, peeking out from under the bed, and her lesson plans, spread across the doily-clad dresser, should have looked out of place in this ultra-feminine setting. But she'd grown up in this room, dreamed in that bed.

The thought pinched. Their last bout of sex hadn't been the stuff that dreams were made of.

Well, his dreams, absolutely. But she deserved better. She deserved more than wild sex in a pickup truck. She deserved someone to make love to her, gentle and careful and tender.

She threaded her fingers through the hair at the back of his neck. "The bed?"

"Ssh. In a minute."

He could do tender, he told himself firmly. For Rachel. Maybe he couldn't protect her tomorrow, but he could damn well comfort her tonight.

Gently he set her on her feet and kissed the space between her eyebrows.

They twitched together. "You don't have to baby me."

"Okay," he said agreeably. "How about I make love to you instead?" He feathered a kiss against her hair.

She shook her head. "I don't want you doing this just to be kind."

Exasperated, he reached for her hand and placed it over the bulge behind his button fly. "Does this feel like 'kind' to you?"

She stroked him. He bit back a groan. "N-no," she said. "But—"

"Responsible Rachel," he mocked gently. "Why don't you let me take care of things for once?"

She wavered. He could see it in her eyes. It was oddly arousing, that uncertainty in determined, decisive Rachel. He kissed her, using his mouth to seduce, his hands to persuade.

When he lifted his head, her lips were soft and her eyes were cloudy. "I really should—"

"In a minute," he murmured. "Give me one minute."

He spun the time out, second by second, in soft caresses and slow, deep kisses. Her breath sighed against his mouth. Her hands fluttered at his waist before settling on his shoulders. She trembled, and that betraying quiver just about did him in.

He slid off the rest of her clothes and laid her down on the bed. He intended for her to enjoy this. But he was shaken by his own satisfaction in seeing her strong body against the white spread, clean-limbed as a beech tree and warm as cedar. Stripping off his shorts and shirt, he gathered her to him, body to body, heart to heart. She reached for him.

"Ssh," he whispered. "Let me."

Let me take you.

And she did, her eyes drifting shut, as he savored and soothed and aroused. Her skin warmed under his touch. Her muscles flexed and relaxed. And every tiny movement and each indrawn breath that signaled her pleasure doubled his.

He lingered and she yielded like a willow bending to the persuasion of the wind. Until the rhythm took him, too, until he was drawn along on her rising pleasure, immersed in every ripple, every quiver of her body. He worked his way back up her damp torso. She danced under him. Swayed around him. He wanted her. He needed her. In one smooth rush, he entered her. And she received him so deeply and completely, he was rooted in the same earth, shaken by the same storm.

He'd never said the three words that would bind a woman to him. He didn't say them now. But he showed her the best way he knew how, each joining a commitment, each stroke a pledge. Their hands met, their fingers twined on the pillow by her head.

"Now," he commanded.

Again. Forever.

Rachel felt him, deep and deeper, pressing into her body, piercing her heart. Always before, in her self-denying generosity, she'd been able to keep back a little piece of herself. She had no defense against Sean's giving. He lavished her with sensation. Destroyed her with tenderness.

Last night, she'd taken her freedom. Tonight, she gave him her heart.

She shattered around him, and he poured himself into her.

Chapter 14

"**Y**ou sound stuffy," Rachel said, worried. She tucked the phone against her ear. "Are you coming down with a cold?"

"M'mouth full." Chris gulped. "Jack's dad made pancakes."

Rachel glanced at the kitchen clock. Nine-twenty. Forty minutes until she needed to be at the high school to deliver sixty-four-thousand counterfeit dollars to a small-time crook. And while she didn't think her nervous stomach could handle a single pancake, she wanted more than anything to be with her children right now. "Am I interrupting breakfast?"

"'S'okay," Chris said cheerfully. "Mr. MacNeill said he'd make me some more. He's really cool, Mom."

So her son was happy with the self-sufficient, magnificent MacNeills. He didn't need her. "That's wonderful, honey."

"I like it here at lot."

"I'm glad."

And she tried to be glad as Chris rattled on about the games he'd played and the video he'd watched and the MacNeills' trampoline. At least, she was grateful. Her children were safe and happy. And her mother was with them, so if anything happened today... Don't go there, she ordered herself.

"My pancakes are ready," Chris announced. "You want to talk to Lindsey?"

"Yes, please. I love you," she said.

The phone crashed. She could hear Chris shouting, and Kate MacNeill's assured voice.

She wrapped her hand in the phone cord until it dug into her skin. As her fingers turned blue, Sean strolled into the kitchen, all lean male grace and pirate stubble, and her stomach went *ka-whump*.

"Mom? You there?" Lindsey asked.

Rachel yanked her hand free from the coils. "I'm here."

"When are you coming to get us?"

She jerked her attention from Sean's torso—this morning his T-shirt read Carpenters Swing Big Tools—and focused on her daughter's question.

"Not until this afternoon, honey."

"But I want to come home now."

Anxiety spiked Rachel's voice. "Is everything all right?"

"I guess. There's nothing to do."

"Did you like the movie?"

"It was gross. They cut open this alien and all this stuff gushed out. Can't I come home now? I miss you."

Even knowing her daughter was pushing her buttons didn't stop the guilt. "I miss you, too. But I have things to do this morning."

"I won't get in the way."

Rachel was shaken. "Sweetheart, I know. But—"

Sean came close and plucked the receiver from her. "Hey, dollface. You check on Hairball for me this morning?"

Rachel, in the act of grabbing back the phone, stopped when he smiled and shook his head.

"Fuzzball, then. But I draw the line at Puffy. Talk to Kate about what supplies we need, okay?"

He listened. Laughed. "Fine. Now tell your mom you love her, and we'll see you after lunch."

Lindsey's voice floated from the receiver, sounding quite cheerful again. "Love you, Mom."

Rachel swallowed the ache in her throat. "I love you."

Sean hung up, and the connection with her children was lost.

"All right?" he asked quietly, watching her face.

She would not cry, Rachel vowed. "Fine."

"That wasn't goodbye," Sean said, surprising her by his perception. "You'll see them in a couple of hours."

She smiled weakly. "I know."

He cupped her shoulders and drew her to him. She let her forehead drop against his chest, let him knead the tension in her neck.

"Rachel...let me come with you."

She fought the terrible temptation to say yes. "He said to come alone."

"I'm not police. I'm no threat. I'm a known quantity— the live-in boyfriend. He won't care if I'm there."

"Lee Gowan said it was safer if no one went with me."

"Safer for Gowan, maybe." His gaze was dark and intense. "Rachel, let me come."

"I can't risk it," she whispered.

I can't risk you, her heart cried. There were some gambles she still wasn't prepared to take.

Sean watched as Rachel backed her mother's Buick carefully down the driveway, her one-way radio clipped to the sun visor, the sack of phony money with the transmitter inside on the seat beside her. Like an anxious parent seeing his only child off to school, he'd made sure she had everything she needed.

Except him.

He frowned as her car slid into the dappled sunshine and down the street. She shouldn't have to face Bilotti alone. Sean didn't care that Gowan had told him to keep his nose out. It didn't matter that Rachel herself wanted him to stay away. He couldn't shake the feeling that he should have gone with her.

Illogical, his brother Con would argue, but Sean had never let logic stand in his way. Patrick would expect him to obey orders. But Sean had always broken the rules.

And he'd never been any damn good at walking away from a fight.

He stomped toward his truck. He should know better. Hell, he did know better. The last time he'd taken on an unwilling woman's troubles, he'd ended up with his heart broken and egg on his face.

Calling himself six kinds of chump, he gunned the engine and headed for the high school.

Rachel squinted as she drove. The sun glared through the windshield. Above the arching trees, the sky was bright with promise. There was nothing menacing about the one-story houses along the road with their rural mailboxes and yard art, concrete deer and feeding geese. There was nothing creepy in the quiet fields, only cows and crows and yellowing tobacco.

When the phone chirped on the seat beside her, she jumped as if an unruly senior had pulled the fire alarm in the middle of end-of-grade testing. Foolish. The children were safe at the MacNeills'. Sean—she squashed her yearning for his solid, reassuring presence—must be back in his workshop by now, and she was on her way to getting the Bilottis out of her life forever. It was stupid to panic just because Lee Gowan was calling to check on her.

She dug for the phone with one hand, swerving slightly to avoid some pancaked roadkill by the centerline. "Hello?"

"Do you have the money with you?"

Panic leaped into her throat and blocked her breathing. She knew that voice. Oh, God, she knew it. It didn't belong to Lee Gowan.

"Do you hear me?" Carmine Bilotti asked.

She moistened her lips. Her eyes sought out the radio hidden above the sun visor. *She* could hear him, yes. But no one else did. "I can hear you."

"So, do you have it or not?"

The money. "Yes."

"Good. Turn left on Powell Road."

A turn would take her away from the high school. Away from the agreed-upon drop and the watching, waiting agents. "Why?"

"You arguing with me, Mrs. Fuller?"

"No."

Do whatever he tells you, Gowan had instructed her. Hands shaking, she turned left across an empty lane as slowly and cautiously as the little old lady she hoped she lived to be. *We'll be there to help.* But now the agent's assurances were no help at all, because every yard she drove took her farther out of range.

He was only following her as far as Old Graham Road, Sean told himself. Less than a mile from the school. They'd pass whoever the FBI had posted at the intersection, and then he'd get his shiny, red, conspicuous butt off the road.

The sun glinted off the roof of Myra Jordan's Buick as it climbed the hill ahead of him. Rachel drove like a kid with her first license, Sean noted with sharp empathy, slowing cautiously as she approached the intersection, signaling her turn. He slowed, too. He didn't want her to see him and worry.

Signaling her turn?

Why was she turning? Powell Road led out of town toward old farms and new construction. Rachel had no business going out that way. Unless the drop had been changed, and she'd decided to keep it from him.

Sean's jaw tightened. She hadn't told him. It pricked his pride. She didn't trust him even that much. But more than his pride was hurting. Rachel's deception bruised his heart. Hadn't she said she had faith in his judgment? Hadn't she let him love her with all that was in him? How could she do that and then lie to him?

Unless she hadn't lied.

Fear blew cold on the back of his neck. Unless something had gone wrong.

Damn, damn, damn. His fingers drummed the wheel. He could push on to Old Graham Road and hope the sight of his bright red truck provoked Gowan's men into revealing themselves and demanding an explanation. Or he could turn, trail Rachel to wherever she was going and hope like hell his tag-along presence didn't put her in even more danger.

He reached the intersection. Rachel's car was nowhere in sight.

He turned left onto Powell Road.

Sweet Mother in Heaven, pray for us.

Clutching the wheel, Rachel steered the car through another swooping curve. Her neck ached from clamping the phone. As she turned, it nearly slithered from beneath her jaw. She grabbed at it while the car drifted from the double yellow line to the narrow shoulder.

"You still there?" Carmine Bilotti demanded.

"I'm here," she muttered.

She was not going to run her car off the road. She would survive. She would not deprive her fatherless children of their mother, too.

At least, she hoped not.

"You over the bridge yet?"

What bridge? "No."

"I want you to keep talking," Carmine said. "I want to know you're on the line."

So she wouldn't be able to hang up the phone. Her neck was breaking, and she couldn't call Gowan for instructions or Sean for support. She sucked on her fear like a nickel in her mouth, flat and metallic-tasting. "What if we get out of my calling area?"

"You're not going that far."

"Well, what if we get cut off?"

"You better hope we don't. I know where your children are, Mrs. Fuller."

Her breath caught. Well, that squelched any thought she had of turning back. Was Frank ahead somewhere waiting for her? Or behind her waiting for Carmine's instructions?

She clung to the memory of Sean's words. *They'll be safe at Patrick's. He's a former marine. My sister-in-law's a doctor.*

Oh, God, what if they needed a doctor?

She bit the inside of her lip, hard. Hysterics wouldn't help. She needed to think. She needed to let Gowan know what had happened. She needed...the radio.

The road echoed beneath her tires.

She cleared her throat. "I just went over the bridge on Powell Road," she said tentatively to the visor above her head. Would Gowan follow her directions? "Where am I going?"

"No names," Carmine warned her. "I'll let you know when you get there."

"How much farther?" she pressed, anxious for any clue that would help Gowan track her down. Would he come right after her? Or wait until she stopped moving?

"I'll tell you. You tell me when you get to the, uh, the water tower thing." Even through the distorted connection, Rachel could hear his disgust. "Jeez, what directions. What did you want to move to Dogpatch for?"

She drove.

"Talk to me," Carmine reminded her sharply.

Anger licked at her. She welcomed it, used it. "I moved to get away from you. Will Frank be...wherever it is I'm going?"

"No names," Carmine repeated. "You keep your eyes peeled now for a big white-and-black sign. For Sale sign. Thirty-seven godforsaken acres for sale."

"I don't see it."

"Keep looking."

There. Up ahead, on her right, white against a screen of dark pines, a painted sign announced the suitability of thirty-seven acres for development.

"I'm there. A big black-and-white Land For Sale sign."

"Okay. Turn right."

"Turn where?"

Carmine swore. "I don't know where. There's some little road. Find it."

She had to turn around, executing a sloppy three-point turn across the double yellow line, but eventually she found it, a rutted construction road cut through red clay and trees.

Doubt clutched at her. Sean could drive it in his truck. But she was in her mama's aging Buick, and every yard down this particular road took her farther into danger.

"I can't drive down there."

"So, park."

She pulled up as close to the turnoff as she dared. Maybe someone would see her parked car and stop?

Not likely. Out here, abandoned cars were lawn decoration, as common as satellite dishes.

The heat shimmered on the empty road. There was a gleam at the top of the hill behind her, but no cars passed. No rescue came.

"Get out of the car," Carmine ordered in her ear. "Take the money with you."

Her chest squeezed. She did not want to leave the car. She didn't want to leave the radio.

What if it wasn't working?

"I don't want to get out," she said directly to her sun visor. "There's nothing here. It's a construction site."

"All you got to do is drop off the money, Mrs. Fuller, and it's all over. Get out of the car."

Do whatever he tells you, Gowan had said. Slowly, she got out of the car.

"Now what?"

"You got the money?"

She reached inside for the brown grocery bag, picking it up from the bottom. Gowan had told her they might be able to lift prints from the top. She readjusted the phone at her ear. "I have the money."

"Down the road, there's some big concrete pipes. Leave the bag inside one of them."

Yes. The transmitter in the bag would lead Lee Gowan to whomever picked up the money. She wouldn't have to face Frank Bilotti at all. Rachel closed her eyes a moment against the flood of relief. She wanted the man arrested. She wanted the threats against her children's lives, her mother's home, stopped. But she was shamefully glad she didn't have to encounter him in this deserted place.

"Should I bring the phone?" she asked Carmine.

"Yeah. I want you to stay on the line."

With the cell phone in one hand and the grocery bag clutched in her other arm, Rachel began to pick her way along the rutted ground. The broken clay had hardened in the heat, making walking difficult. The thin line of trees gave way to orange netting and stakes tied with strips of pink and blue plastic. Bulldozers had shaped and gouged the earth into huge hills and street beds. The sun beat down. A dog barked in the distance.

You'll look like you're on your own. You'll feel like you're on your own, but you won't be.

She'd feel a whole lot better with Sean beside her. Safer, under the protection of his ready strength and quick possessiveness, his dangerous looks and big, scarred hands.

Don't go there, she told herself firmly. She could handle this without him—and without his getting hurt. She would handle this, leave the money and go home, and then everyone she loved would be safe.

The broken roadbed wandered up a rise to a stand of forlorn trees, skinny pines and hickories shaped like toilet brushes, wrapped in orange plastic fence. Beside the trees, two bulldozers and a crane stood watch over a stockpile of concrete drainpipes, each big enough for a child to stand in.

Sweat broke out on Rachel's upper lip. This was it. She could drop the bag now and run.

She left the half road and made her way to the culverts. Clay crunched and pebbles rolled beneath her feet. It was quiet here. So quiet, and too hot. A warm breeze blew grit over her shoes and plastered a lunch wrapper against a pipe.

She put the hand that held the phone on the upper lip of the opening, for balance. Crouching, she took two steps inside. The concrete interior was dark and dank and still. A brackish puddle stained the bottom. She misjudged it in the shadows and stepped right in, wetting her shoes. Ugh. Setting the bag down high on one side—did the FBI reuse conterfeit?—she backed out.

Behind her, a deep voice rasped, "Looks like special-delivery time."

Her heart hurtled into her throat. She turned, blinking against the sun.

Frank Bilotti leaned against the flat yellow side of the crane, picking his teeth with his thumbnail and watching her.

"Yeah." His gaze crawled over her simple white blouse, her legs below the hem of her plain khaki shorts. "I'd say real special."

Her stomach pushed up to join her heart. She was going to be sick.

No, she wasn't.

Rachel moistened her lips. "Frank's here," she said into the phone.

"Frankie?" Carmine's voice rose in surprise. "What the hell is that dumb bastard doing there?"

Frank took two swift strides over the ground. Rachel flinched from his reaching hand, but he only grabbed the phone.

"It's okay, Uncle Carmine. I got it."

He listened a moment, his brow lowering, his lip twisting in anger. "I told you, I'm taking care of things now," he said, and pressed the little button that cut off Rachel's last connection with the world.

The fear was back and rising. "Your uncle didn't expect you to be here."

Frank Bilotti smiled. Not a nice smile. She shuddered. "I bet you didn't either, huh, teacher lady? It's not like country living is my style. I hate it down here. Cows. I hate cows and dirt. I don't like getting dirty."

Rachel raised her chin a notch. "Too bad, given your line of work."

He scowled. "The way I figure it, you owe me something for my trouble."

Oh, God, he didn't mean... No, she reassured herself. The Bilottis were businessmen.

"The money is in there. I put it in the pipe."

"I saw you. Get it out."

She was a hundred yards from her car. She could run, but he might catch her. Or he might be armed. She turned and ducked and, conscious of his watching eyes, retrieved the heavy brown paper sack from the culvert.

She held it out to him. "Here."

He jerked his head toward the bulldozers. "Over there. Put it in my car."

His car must be parked out of sight. Uneasiness curdled her stomach. "I think I should go now."

He reached behind him, and a gun appeared in his hand, blunt and dull, with a black hole like a blind eye staring at her. "And I think you should do what I say."

She thought so, too. He didn't even have to shoot to rob her of breath. Of courage. Her hope leaked out the bottom of her wet shoes. Bilotti could take the money and run, and the transmitter would continue to signal the location of the money pack. But if he shot and dumped her, it could be tomorrow before anyone discovered her body.

Oh, Chris. Lindsey. I'm so sorry, babies.

Where the hell was Gowan?

But it wasn't the federal agent Rachel yearned for. It was Sean MacNeill. She mocked her heart's hope, her stubborn, foolish faith. She'd told him and told him to leave her alone. What could he do against a gun, anyway?

Get shot, she answered her own question. There was nothing he could do but make things worse.

And in the end, there was nothing she could do but go where the gun pointed.

"On the front seat. That's right." Frank smirked. "Now you get in back."

Fear froze her legs. Anger stiffened her spine. "Why?"

"You want to strip out here?"

"No. That wasn't the deal. I never agreed to—" rape, she thought sickly "—to go with you."

"The only place you're going is the back seat. Move it."

Dear Lord. Her mind almost shut down from terror. *The only place you're going...* Was he going to shoot her, then, when he was done with her?

"Why don't you just take the money and go?"

His free hand stroked his belt. "I figure you owe me a

more personal payment first. I'm gonna teach you some respect.''

She battled for breath, struggled for arguments that might save her. "We—you don't have time. What if I'm being followed?"

"Carmine figured you might be. That's why he switched the drop. Nobody's following you. Unless..." His pumpkin head shifted on his blocky shoulders. "You wearing a wire, teacher lady?''

Was that movement, on the other side of the bulldozer?

"No," she said loudly.

Bilotti took a step closer. His gun traced the line of her buttons. "Lemme see."

Her gaze darted behind him and back, desperate for rescue, desperate to hold his attention. "I told you, no."

"And I told you to do what I say. Now, are you going to take off that pretty blouse or am I?''

If he touched her, she would vomit. Had she imagined that flicker of movement, conjured it from dust and heat and fear?

No. There! The toe of a boot, a man's brown work boot. A glimpse of dark hair...

Sean.

Joy geysered through her. And then fear struck to her bones.

What could he do against a gun? Get shot.

She had to distract Bilotti. As slowly as she dared, she began to unbutton her shirt, not bothering to hide her trembling. Maybe her shaking hands would excuse her delay.

Burning with rage and shame, she let the blouse hang open. She didn't dare look in the direction of the bulldozer again. "See? No wire."

Bilotti licked his lips. "I see, all right. Nice. Get in the car."

She was strong. She could fight him.

And get shot? Or risk Sean getting shot?

No. She couldn't gamble his safety on her clumsy self-defense. She would not force her children to bury their mother. Her job was to survive. Whatever it took.

With his free hand, Bilotti opened the rear door of the car. "Hurry it up." He grinned. "I got a special delivery for you, too."

Tears burned in her eyes. Damn it. Damn him.

She climbed into the back seat. Bilotti came in after her.

"Real nice," he said, and grabbed her breast.

She forced herself not to resist, forced herself not to cry out in protest.

He lowered her onto the seat and crawled between her thighs; paused, to stick the gun in the back of his waistband.

"Now," she croaked.

He smirked. "In a hurry, aren't you?"

The window behind him darkened as something—someone—leaned against it. The door pressed in, pinning his legs as they hung out of the car. Bilotti yelled.

Rachel scrambled backward, kicking. With a hand on her chest, he shoved her down. The other reached behind him for his gun.

She looked past his head at the window. White shirt, dark hair...

"No!" she screamed as Bilotti twisted and fired over his shoulder.

Flash. Bang. The gunshot, echoing in the close interior of the car, nearly deafened her. Sean disappeared from the opening as pebbles of glass showered inward. Rachel turned her face away.

Was he safe? Shot? She struggled to see.

Bilotti levered himself up with an elbow on her stomach. She grunted and bucked against his weight.

He jerked his gun hand around. ''Bitch.'' The muzzle wavered, seeking her.

Sobbing, she curled into the door, kicking out at him. Her foot struck his arm. The gun fired. Pain exploded in her ears, but it was only sound. The bullet ripped through the roof, leaving black powder burns on the gray lining.

The door pinning Bilotti's legs jerked open. Sean's big hands, his strong arms, heaved Bilotti off her and dragged him from the car. She heard the thump and howl as his chin hit the jamb of the door, saw the gun wave over his head.

She reached for the door handle that dug into her back, felt the catch release and tumbled from the car. She staggered and ran behind the trunk to the other side.

She saw work boots and jeans and blood. Lots of blood. Sean's blood? Her heart stopped. He sprawled on top of Bilotti, the two men scrabbling for position like a pair of high school wrestlers. Only Bilotti's gun arm was pinned above his head, and the back of Sean's white shirt was dark with blood.

He was hit. He was hurt. A new, raw terror froze her heart, her lungs, her legs.

Time crawled.

Gowan should be here.

He wasn't coming.

Bilotti heaved, and more blood seeped into Sean's shirt. She sobbed. ''Oh, God. Oh, God. What can I do?''

''Stomp on his hand,'' Sean directed tersely. ''Get the gun.''

She ran around their feet and scuttled along the inside of the door, her eyes fixed on Sean's left shoulder, on the ominous spread of blood. His right arm stretched over Bilotti's, clamping his forearm. Bilotti's knuckles were white with his efforts to free the gun.

The gun.

The gun he'd used to shoot Sean.

She raised her right foot and stomped on the back of his hand.

The gun fired under the car. She screamed. Bilotti grunted as Sean brought his knee up into his back.

"Harder," Sean ordered hoarsely.

Was he paler now? She took a sharp breath and ground her heel into the gunman's hand.

He yowled. His fingers splayed. She kicked the gun away, under the car.

"Bitch," Bilotti moaned. "You broke my hand."

"Good," she spat.

Sean laughed weakly.

Oh, God. He was still bleeding. She ripped off her blouse to staunch the flow of blood.

Falling to her knees in the dirt beside him, she heard the rev of motors, the crunch of gravel. One car? Two? Doors slammed. Men's voices raised. She pressed her shirt against Sean's wound. He needed help. More help than she could give him. With a desperate glance behind her, she staggered to her feet and around the crane.

A dark sedan parked at the edge of the roadbed. A sleek pickup bounced toward it through the ruts. Four men in dark jackets ran over the uneven ground, kicking up red dust with every stride.

Rachel waved frantically, not caring that she was only wearing a bra and shorts. Her shirt was wadded against Sean's shoulder.

"Hold on," she begged him. "It's Lee Gowan."

Bilotti cursed.

Sean turned his ashen face to grin crookedly over his shoulder. "Guess the cavalry made it after all."

He slumped, unconscious, just as Gowan arrived.

Rachel sobbed. Sean had rescued her from the devil, and delivered her into hell.

Chapter 15

Sean was no stranger to hospitals. Between his nephew's accident, his father's stroke a couple years back, and his sister-in-law's job, he'd done his time in lounges and cafeterias. Sean didn't mind the waiting. He could even handle the coffee.

But all that was different from lying on a hard bed and a flat pillow with a plastic line running into his arm. He hurt. His throat ached from the tube they'd stuck down him before operating to remove the bullet from his shoulder joint. His right arm was tight and swollen around the IV, and his left shoulder hurt like a son of a bitch despite the drugs pumping through him. He couldn't eat yet. He couldn't sleep. Hell, he could barely make it to the bathroom by himself, trundling along with his IV pole and the hospital gown flapping around his butt.

Sean grinned at the acoustic tiles above his head. All things considered, he felt pretty good.

He felt like a goddamn hero.

"You acted like a goddamn fool, getting shot," Con had told him, while Patrick nodded in grim agreement.

But it didn't matter any longer what his brothers thought. All that mattered was that Rachel was safe.

Safe, but not with him.

Sean shifted on the unforgiving mattress, trying to find a comfortable position with his arm strapped to his chest. He understood that, after all the excitement, Rachel needed to get her children settled in their own beds last night. He knew she had classes to teach today.

He'd been aware of and grateful for her presence yesterday evening: her hand cool on his forehead, her lips warm on his cheek. He'd carried her scent with him into sleep, and when he'd opened his eyes the first thing he'd seen had been her dark hair loose around her pale, worried face.

She didn't have to worry anymore. He was fine. Everything was going to be fine. It was stupid to feel lonely.

The bed next to his was empty, but the friendly nurses made regular checks on his room. Sean smiled at the ceiling. Very friendly nurses. Very regular checks. Lee Gowan came to take a statement. Not a social call, that, but welcome all the same, since it helped put the Bilottis away.

And the MacNeills rallied, as always, around the fallen of the clan. Con and Val had been by twice, last night and this morning. Kate used her doctor privileges to sit with him after visiting hours, and Patrick had brought Jack in to see him. Jack, a hospital veteran, brought his uncle hard candy and an electronic baseball game. When his parents called, Sean barely talked Bridget out of flying down to nurse him, and even big taciturn John MacNeill got on the phone to hear for himself that their youngest son was all right.

Sean had no grounds for missing Rachel. But he did.

The door opened, and she was there like an answer to his prayers, grave and beautiful as an angel in a stained-glass window. She must have come directly from school. She was still in teacher clothes, a long skirt and navy pumps. He smiled with pure pleasure at seeing her.

She smiled back uncertainly. "They told me you were asleep."

"More like stuck in bed." He twitched back a corner of the sheet. "Want to join me?"

She shook her head, but she sat by the bed, close enough that he could smell her perfume. "I never thanked you for yesterday."

He started to shrug; grimaced instead as the movement pulled his shoulder. "I didn't do anything."

"You got shot."

"That didn't help you any."

"Stop fishing. You were wonderful, and you know it. You *followed* me."

The disbelief in her voice made him frown. "You kept your head. You left the car where I could see it."

"If you hadn't come when you did—"

"Yeah, and if the FBI hadn't come when they did—"

She sat up straighter. "You already had Bilotti on the ground."

"And you kicked his gun away."

Momentary pleasure sparkled in her eyes, banishing the guilt. "Only because you told me to."

"So, we make a good team."

"I don't think crime fighting is in my future," Rachel said dryly.

Her future. Yes. Funny how the word had always made him squirm. Now all he could think was how bleak his future would be without her in it.

"I'm no superhero, either," he said.

The glow in her eyes made him feel as though he had a big red *S* on his chest instead of surgical tape and a bandage.

"Hero enough," she said simply.

He was caught between pleasure and embarrassment. "I hope I've got what it takes to make you happy, anyway."

"Sean, I—"

"Wait a minute." Damned if he'd say his next bit lying flat on his back. He struggled to sit up. His shoulder screamed in protest, and he fumbled for the control that would raise the bed.

"Are you all right?" Rachel asked anxiously.

"Fine," he lied. Sweat broke on his upper lip. He could release another dose of painkiller into his IV, but he didn't want to make the biggest decision of his life whacked out on morphine.

He dropped the control and took her hand, cursing the lack of two good arms. "Look, maybe neither one of us is cut out for battling bad guys. But we did it together. We're good together."

"We are. But—"

"Now that this is over, I want us to stay together."

"*Oh.*" Real distress pulled at the corners of her mouth. Her hand trembled in his. "I never meant… I just came to thank you."

He kissed her fingertips. What was she upset about? "Thanking me is good. You can thank me any way you want. Of course, this bed's a little small, but—"

"We shouldn't be having this discussion now. You're hurt."

"Wounded, but functional." When she didn't smile, unease stirred in his gut. "What is it?"

"I don't want to fight with you."

He tried to joke. "Won't make love, won't fight... What's left?"

She looked wretched. "Nothing. Nothing's left."

"What are you talking about?"

She tugged her hand away. Folded it in her lap. "I'm not like you. I'm a steady, boring person. I want a steady, boring life. I can't live with the highs and lows. When I saw you lying there... I never want to be so frightened again."

Panic, compounded by sleeplessness and pain, roughened his voice. "That's stupid. You'd be frightened—and a hell of a sight worse—if I hadn't shown up."

"I know that. I told you, I'm grateful."

"I don't want your damn gratitude."

"I can't give you anything else. I have the children to think of. They're just getting over their father's death. He killed himself, for heaven's sake. And then you getting shot... It's too soon, don't you see?"

"That's bull. The kids and I do fine."

Her eyes pleaded with him to understand. "They need stability."

He understood better than she knew. "No. That's what you think you need."

"What if I do?"

"Then you're wrong. You need me." Needed him to be there for her, to pledge her his life and his heart and his strength. Why didn't she see that?

"*Need* you?" she asked.

He didn't like her tone. Damn it, *he* needed *her*. She was the other half of him, the solid center of his world, the brisk wind that gave wings to his dreams. Impatient with her denial, he said rashly, "You never had it so good."

Her chin snapped up. "The sex has never been so good, if that's what you mean. Is that what you want to hear?"

"It'll do for a start."

She was working herself into a fine, feminine temper now. "There's more to my life than sex."

"Hell, don't I know that? Isn't that what I'm trying to be part of? But I can't do it if you won't let me in."

"I can't!" she cried. "I can't let you in and live with the fear of losing you."

The way she'd lost her father. The way she'd lost her husband. The way she'd lost Uncle Jed and all the men who'd come and gone in her childhood.

Stubbornly, Sean repeated, "I'm not going anywhere."

She turned his own words back against him. "You might not have a choice."

"Maybe when they let me out of here, I should just go to my brother's," he challenged her.

Her lips trembled. She pressed them together. "Maybe that would be best."

She stood. She couldn't be *leaving*.

She was.

"Rachel!"

She turned politely at the door, her face a mask of misery.

What could he do, Sean thought in panic, what could he say, to convince her to stay? He'd always been good with words and better with women, but her distress and determination wiped his mind as blank as a primed wall. And so he spoke the first, and possibly the worst, words that came to his unwary tongue. "You're making a big mistake."

Her shoulders were rigid. "It's my mistake to make."

"But it's all of us who will live with the consequences."

She had nothing to say to that. The door closed silently behind her, leaving him alone with his splinted shoulder and his broken heart.

Chump.

Myra shook a dish towel from the laundry basket that sat on the kitchen table. "You haven't been to the hospital today, dear."

Guilt and longing lashed Rachel. Grabbing one of Chris's shirts, she folded it tightly into a precise square. "I went yesterday. And I called today to see how Sean was doing. The nurse said he didn't have a fever. He can go home tomorrow."

"Why don't you go tonight? See for yourself."

It was too tempting. Sean would look at her with his shrewd dark eyes and touch her with his big hard hands and she'd forget all her good intentions and give him anything he wanted. Everything she wanted. And then when he didn't want any more, her heart would be shattered and her children would be bewildered and her mother would want her to take up with the next man who passed by.

No.

"I don't like to leave the children," Rachel said, taking refuge in more laundry. More lies. "They're still upset about this weekend."

Myra tutted. "Chris had a wonderful time. And Lindsey's only angry because you didn't tell her what was happening, not because you left them with the MacNeills."

"They're still my responsibility. I'm not going to ask you to baby-sit again."

"Then take them. They want to see Sean, too."

"I don't want them to get too attached to him."

"It may be too late for that," Myra said.

Rachel was afraid her mother was right. She thought of Chris's excitement over the family ball game, Lindsey's comfort in the kitten, Sean's patience with them both. "They'll get over it."

"Probably. But will you?"

"I'll have to, won't I?"

Myra sighed. "I suppose. And you'll probably be better at it than I was. Though I really thought the children liked Sean. You were so close to your father, I never felt it was fair to ask you to accept another man in your life."

"There were a lot of men, Mama."

"Yes," Myra agreed simply. "I used to get so lonely." She added with pride, "But I never *married* any of them."

Rachel felt as though one of the socks had just turned around and bit her. "Wait a minute. They asked?"

Myra patted her hair. "From time to time. But of course I said no."

Rachel's brain whirled. "Because of me," she said slowly. "You didn't marry because you wanted to protect me?"

It was a tough concept to wrap her thoughts around. All this time she'd worried about repeating her mother's mistakes by indulging in a fleeting affair. Think of the children, she'd told herself. Protect the children. And all the time Myra Jordan believed she had done the same.

Rachel had repeated her mother's mistakes after all, and the realization made her sick. She bowed her head over the laundry basket. She'd projected her fears of abandonment onto her children so that she wouldn't have to examine her own feelings and failings too closely.

And Sean had seen it. Sean had known.

Who are we talking about here? he'd argued.

That's what you think you need.

You are so afraid of losing you can't win.

"You're my daughter," Myra said simply. "I always put you first."

Rachel's eyes stung. She bent to hug the short, soft, wrong-headed woman sitting at the kitchen table. "Oh, Mama. I do love you."

"I love you, too," Myra said.

Rachel hesitated. "Was there ever anyone that you…"

"Wanted?" Her mother's eyes slid away. "I suppose. Jed Peeler from church… But that was too soon after your father died. Jed didn't want to wait, and I didn't want to hurt you. And after that, I just didn't let myself think that way."

Uncle Jed and her mother. Rachel struggled with the might-have-beens and then gave up. She couldn't blame her mother for her decisions.

But she could reexamine her own.

If he couldn't have Rachel, he should at least be allowed to drink.

Sean sat on the front porch swing, his shoulder trussed and aching. He watched his brothers tip back long-necked bottles of beer, and his sense of unfairness grew.

Val intercepted his brooding look and smiled. "Get you one?" she offered.

Kate shook her head. "Not with the Vicodin he's taking."

Con reached out a long arm to pull his wife down beside him. "She's pregnant, anyway. She shouldn't be fetching for you. Get your own woman to wait on you."

"I tried," Sean said shortly. "She wasn't interested."

Con raised his eyebrows. "Uh-oh."

Kate asked quietly, "How is Rachel?"

Patrick set down his bottle with a decisive clink. "She's fine. He's the one who got shot."

Val addressed the porch in general. "I just love it when he does the protective big brother routine, don't you?"

Sean ignored her. "Rachel's doing all right."

"Did they arrest the other man? The one in Philadelphia?" Kate pressed.

"They got him. According to Gowan, Frank's busy talking himself out of the extortion charge, and Carmine's trying to convince the feds shooting at us was all his nephew's idea. They should have enough to put both Bilottis away for a long time."

"How are the kids?" Patrick asked.

"The kids are fine. Rachel is fine. Her life is back in its safe little rut, and she has everything she ever wanted." Sean glared around belligerently. "Which, since you all are so interested in my private life, does not include me."

Not unsympathetically, Con asked, "Feeling sorry for yourself, are you?"

"Hell, no. Who needs her? Who needs any of it? She used me." Just like Trina had.

"Used you, how?"

"Like some stupid bodyguard." It hurt.

"But you said she told you not to follow her," Con argued logically. "The feds told you not to follow her. That Bureau guy, that Gowan, he sounded ticked that you were there at all."

He was right. Sean hunched his one good shoulder. "Yeah, well, she doesn't want anything to do with me now."

Kate frowned. "She wouldn't leave your side at the hospital. That certainly suggests that she cares about you."

The memory of Rachel's soothing touch dug into Sean like a knife. "Well, she doesn't," he muttered.

"Yeah, I could tell all along she was just interested in your body," Con drawled.

"It was more than that," Sean snarled. "I thought she had faith in me. That's what bites. That after everything, she didn't—doesn't—trust me not to let her down."

"Because you asked her to marry you and she refused," Val probed delicately.

"Yeah, I... That is, I didn't exactly propose."

Con raised his eyebrows. "But you told her you loved her."

Sean tried to remember. "I think I did."

"Oh, brother."

The two women exchanged glances.

"Let me get this straight," said Patrick. "You want this woman to trust you with her future and her kids, but you didn't tell her you love her or that you want to marry her."

Put like that, it sounded bad. Fear touched him. "That wasn't how it was," Sean protested.

"He blew it," Con decided. "Mr. Fast-Talk-Fast-Hands blew it."

"I think it's sweet," Val said.

Sean panicked. Had he really screwed up? "Sweet, my—"

"Watch it," Patrick said mildly.

Sean hauled himself up. The swing banged against the wall. He was a turnip head. An idiot. With all the disappointments in her past, Rachel needed reassurance more than most women. How could he have been so blind? "I've got to go to her. I've got to tell her—"

"You may not have to go anywhere," Kate said. "Look."

He didn't recognize the car nosing up the long drive, but he thought he knew that cautious turn, the law-abiding speed.

His heart slammed into his chest in sudden, awful hope.

In a rented late-model Ford, Rachel Fuller was lurching back into his life. He could only pray she'd give him the chance to be a part of hers.

Rachel surveyed the assembled MacNeills, her courage crawling into her shoes. They were all there on the porch to welcome Sean home: cool Con and his beautiful, pregnant wife; Patrick, stiff with protective pride; Kate, with worry in her eyes. Their unstated message was clear.

To get to him, she had to go through them.

She wanted to tell them she was no threat to their solid family circle. She was here to make her case and go. Whatever happened after that was up to Sean.

She hitched up her resolution. She'd brought reinforcements of her own, hadn't she? Or at least, she thought with a twist of bleak humor, her own camp followers.

"Okay, troops." She shifted into park. "Let's get out of the car."

"Where's Sean?" Lindsey asked.

"I see him!" Chris shouted.

There. Standing tall in the shelter of the porch, in the shadow of the swing. He hadn't shaved, and his arm was held tight to his chest by the blue contraption he'd worn in the hospital. He looked tired, Rachel thought with concern, and so handsome her breath caught.

"We were worried about you," Chris said, running up the porch steps. "Mom said the doctor had to take a bullet out of your shoulder. Did they let you keep it? Can I see?"

Sean caught and hugged him with one arm. "The police

wanted the bullet, sport. But I'll let you count my staples later.''

The boy grinned, reassured. "Cool."

Lindsey stood back, biting her lip. "Are you going to be okay?"

Rachel's throat ached at the tableau they made, the big dark-haired man with the boy at his side, the dark-haired girl anxious and apart.

Sean hunkered down so that he could look Lindsey in the eyes. "Yeah," he said with absolute certainty. "I am."

She nodded once, accepting his honesty. Rachel loved that, that he'd always been straight with her daughter. Lindsey could *trust* him. "Then why aren't you coming home?"

Rachel sucked in her breath. Well, that was honest. Sean looked over Lindsey's head at Rachel as if she had the answer.

Damn. She hadn't counted on quite so many witnesses to her surrender. But neither could she put it off any longer.

"Con," Kate said suddenly. "Why don't you and Val take the children to the barn to check on Fluffy."

"Fuzzball," Sean corrected, never taking his eyes off Rachel. Her heart pounded.

Lindsey giggled.

"We can do that," Con said in an amused voice. He offered a hand to his pregnant wife. They strolled off arm in arm, the children running ahead.

"Patrick, can you give me a hand in the kitchen?" Kate continued.

"You want me to help you in the kitchen?" Patrick repeated carefully. Rachel remembered Kate couldn't— didn't—cook.

She gave him a significant look. "In the house. Now. Please?"

Her husband shrugged. The two of them disappeared inside, but not before Rachel heard Patrick growl, "I suppose you think he's old enough to take care of himself."

Kate's laugh floated back to the porch. "Old enough to know what he wants."

Rachel was alone with Sean. The air was thick with silence. Her palms were damp. She was no gambler, and the stakes were so incredibly high.

She cleared her throat. "I like your sister-in-law."

Sean watched her gravely. "I like her myself."

She wanted to yell at him to come down off that porch and kiss her, to say something outrageous or suggestive, to hold her hard or make her laugh.

She wanted him to make the next step easy for her.

But that wasn't what they both needed, Rachel realized. Some other time, maybe, but not now. Sean needed her to offer herself without strings or qualifications. And she needed to take the risk.

I want us to be together, he'd said, but he wasn't going to make it happen. She would have to take what she wanted, the way she had out on the old logging road, not for one night, but for forever.

Or for however long he was willing to give her.

Oh, help. She put one foot on the steps.

And he came down three.

"Wait a minute," she said. "I'm coming to you."

He stopped, and gave her his slow, sexy pirate's smile, the one that scrambled her brain and liquefied her insides. "So hurry up."

She couldn't stop her answering smile, but she said seriously, "I have something to say first."

He hitched the thumb of his good hand in his pocket. "I'm listening."

"These last couple of days... It's been like this great big weight dropped off my shoulders. No phone threats. No payments. No worrying that some maniac was going to break into my house or stalk my kids." Her smile flickered. "I'm even having heart-to-hearts with my mother."

He waited silently for her to finish her say. She couldn't read his expression, not through the tears that suddenly blurred her eyes.

"But you were right," she told him. "It's not enough. I never had it so good as I did with you. I want you to come back, Sean."

"To the garage."

She moistened her dry lips. "If that's what you want. I meant, to all of us. To me."

"Taking a chance on me, beautiful?" he asked wryly.

"Taking a chance on myself."

He moved then, taking the final step that put them on a level. His right hand lifted and touched her hair in a gesture so sweet she had to close her eyes to keep the tears from spilling.

"You aren't the only one afraid of taking risks, you know."

She opened her eyes. His face swam in her vision, dark and close and tender. "Excuse me?"

"I was holding back on you, too. I didn't want to give you the chance to say no. But I never gave you the words you needed to trust me, either."

She shook her head. He was being kind. She couldn' let herself off the hook so easily. "I should have known— I do know—what kind of a man you are. You don't have to say the words."

"Well, I'm saying them now, damn it." He knelt care

fully, stiffly, because of his shoulder. "I love you, Rachel. Will you marry me?"

She stared at the top of his dark head, taken aback by the old-fashioned courtliness of his gesture. It was totally unexpected. Completely right. She felt giddy.

"You're on your knees," she said. Awed. Overcome. And more in love than she ever would have believed.

"That's how we do it in our family," he explained.

Sean was appalled when she started to cry, great gasping sobs that tore his heart. He lumbered back to his feet. "Rachel...sweetheart... It's okay if you don't feel—"

"No! Oh, no." She shook her head vehemently, her eyes shining. "I love you."

Joy sluiced through him. He put his one good arm around her and held her as tightly as he dared. Her hands curled into his shoulders. He kissed her brow, her cheek, her lips. Her cheeks were wet. He could taste the salt of her tears. Confused, he asked, "Then...is it the kids? Is it too soon? Do you need time to adjust?"

She nestled, trying to get closer despite his sling. "We don't need time. We don't need anything but you."

Powerful words, for a man who'd struggled most of his life to measure up. She knocked him off his feet. But he still didn't understand her.

"Then...what is it?"

"I never thought you would do that," she confessed simply. "I never expected anybody ever to do anything so sweet for me."

He was touched. Amused. And shaken to the heart by her declaration. "Mother in Heaven," he muttered. "What are you going to do when I give you the ring?"

Her smile shone brighter than the gold at the end of the rainbow.

"Wear it," she said. "And tell everyone I won it betting on a sure thing."

Epilogue

There was a man in Rachel's hotel room, in Rachel's bed. A naked man, she guessed, by the hard curve of shoulder that showed in the light from the bathroom. In the dim room, his earring winked like a promise.

Anticipation thrilled through her. She smoothed her palms down white silk, a gift from her sisters-in-law.

She cleared her throat. "It was a nice wedding."

The man in her bed opened his eyes. His dark gaze jolted her heartbeat. A slow smile curved his wide mouth.

"You looked beautiful."

Rachel flushed with pleasure. She'd worn her mother's wedding veil and his grandmother's ring and carried red and white roses. Perfect for a Christmas wedding, Val announced with satisfaction.

Everything had been perfect, Rachel thought. Her bridesmaids—Kate and Val with her new son watching from her husband's arms—wore dark green velvet. Lindsey, as maid of honor, trembled with pride as she walked in front of her mother up the aisle. Best man Chris had charge of the rings up until the moment Sean had said, *Take this ring as a sign of my love and fidelity. In the name of the Father and the Son and the Holy Spirit...*

Sean held his hand out to her now, and her own ring gleamed on his finger.

Without hesitation, she joined her hand with his.

With a tug, he brought her down beside him on the mattress. His warm breath skated across her mouth. He smelled like toothpaste, like soap and sex and man. Her heart was so full of joy she thought she might burst with it, or weep. She smiled instead.

"Welcome home, Rachel MacNeill," Sean said, and folded her into his arms.

* * * * *

presents a riveting 12-book continuity series:

A Year of loving dangerously

Where passion rules and nothing is what it seems...

When dishonor threatens a top-secret agency, the brave
men and women of SPEAR are prepared to risk it all as they
put their lives—and their hearts—on the line.

Available October 2000:

HER SECRET WEAPON

by Beverly Barton

The only way agent Burke Lonigan can protect his pretty
assistant is to offer her the safety of his privileged lifestyle—as
his wife. But what will Burke do when he discovers Callie is
the same beguiling beauty he shared one forgotten night of
passion with—and the mother of his secret child?

*Available only from Silhouette Intimate Moments
at your favorite retail outlet.*

Where love comes alive™

Visit Silhouette at www.eHarlequin.com   SIMAYOLD5

**Don't miss
an exciting opportunity
to save on the purchase of
Harlequin and Silhouette books!**

Buy any two Harlequin or
Silhouette books and save
$10.00 off future Harlequin
and Silhouette purchases

OR

buy any three
Harlequin or Silhouette books
and save **$20.00 off** future
Harlequin and Silhouette purchases.

**Watch for details
coming in October 2000!**

PHQ400

COMING NEXT MONTH